I0547086

Broken 7 Unapologetically Me

Sherlynn Rachelle

Blessed By Faith Publication
IN SPIRIT & IN TRUTH

Copyright © 2016 Sherlynn Rachelle

Broken 7 Unapologetically Me
By Sherlynn Rachelle

Printed in the United States of America

ISBN: 979-8-9862383-0-2

All rights reserved solely by the author. The author
guarantees all contents are original works and do
not infringe upon the legal rights of any other
person or work. The author is not a licensed medical
practitioner or holds any legal title or position. The
views expressed in this book are not the advice of
any medical practitioner or legal authority. The
opinions expressed in this book are not necessarily
those of the publisher. No part of this book may be
reproduced without the author's permission.

Scripture quotations are taken from the public

domain of the King James Version(KJV).

Blessed By Faith Publication Edition 2022

To Give Honor where Honor is Due:

All Praises to God (Yah) first and foremost; thank you, Jesus (Yeshua).

A special thank you to the book cover designer—Gregory Lynn (G.E.L), of Minnesota.

Contents:

Chapter One: My Dream, My Reality

Wren closed her acceptance speech with, *"Growing up without genuine love from parents and other family members could cause any child to have long-lasting depression, fears of rejection, and instability. You will fail if you do not learn to change the negative narrative. This award demonstrates how I changed the negative to positive. I let go of being a product of my childhood environment and persevered to become Wren Davidson, an award-winning celebrity fashion designer, and I am grateful for the change. Thank you, everyone."*

The pouring sounds of rain and the summer breeze set the tone for a relaxed evening of soft music, red wine, and great company. Wren Davidson snuggled in her warm white fluffy blanket. Nights like this were her favorite. She loved to sit back and chill on her coffee-brown lazy boy chair in her sunroom.

The long-awaited award show aired this evening. Wren and her friend Cartel waited weeks to see it. Wren won her first fashion designer of the year award. She had worked so hard to become a celebrity fashion designer. Tonight's award meant everything to her. "Tell me, one more time, Cartel, how did my acceptance speech sound?"

Sitting on the couch across from Wren, Cartel placed a glass of red wine on the table. She stood up and walked over to the chair to join Wren. "Wren, you did fine. If you are concerned about breaking down in tears, do not be. It only helped your fan base to understand your story even more. That is why you received a standing ovation. You deserved this award, which is only up from here, my friend."

Wren's eyes watered as she reflected on her friend's words. She recalled the day her mother got sent to serve a twelve-year prison sentence. *How could she?* Then, her father discovered she and her brother Steven were not his biological children. *How could he?* And finally, the day she and Steven entered the horrific world of foster care. *How could they?* "Do you think Sharon was watching the awards?" Wren asked, Cartel.

"Wren, you know your mother was watching the awards. She wants to reach out to you personally, but she knows better." Cartel responded, moving back to her seat on the couch.

"Well, she should have thought about it before doing what she did. What type of mother does that? Leaving her children behind to be cared for by the world."

"Wren, we have had this conversation so many times. She made a horrible mistake. She spent twelve full years in prison without knowing where her children were. I cannot force myself to believe that if she had known that your father, Daniel, would seek a paternity test, get the results, and throw you two into the system, she would NOT have taken that case for him. She was a loving mother, and you said this yourself."

Wren battled with forgiveness. The shift between foster homes was tough. Somehow, she and her brother Steven managed to stay coupled. The duo became a potent force. They were a comfort to each other's lowest points and celebrated their highest. Under one foster mother's care, Wren learned how to make fast money. By the age of sixteen, she was stripping in nightclubs to make ends meet, inhabiting that lifestyle for over ten years provided - housing, food, and clothing for herself and Steven.

"Steven wants me to forgive her too. He contacted her, but I am not ready."

"Well, do not force it. It will come if you ask the Lord to help you with it. I would give anything to have an opportunity to speak to my parents again."

"The Lord, Cartel! I know I just moved back home to Chicago after being in Los Angeles for five years, but nothing has changed about the so-called Lord and Savior. He still does not exist, so thanks, but I am good on that part."

"Now you know I am not going to listen to that foolishness. That is my queue to go home. I love you, bestie, but you cannot disrespect the Lord. We have been friends long enough to respect boundaries." Cartel rose from the couch.

"Cartel, do not leave so soon. We have not seen each other in so long," Wren acknowledged, sipping her wine. "I am just so grateful that I listened to that inner me. The pull from within would not allow me to stay at the fortune five hundred company. I could not imagine my life complete without conquering this goal."

Wren Davidson and Cartella (Cartel) Markham met in community college; a conversation between the two launched a long-term friendship, twenty years and counting. They both shared mutual social classes. They grew up in foster care as children. Cartel's parents died in a drug deal gone bad. Shortly after, the grandmother who cared for her died from a sudden illness. She had no siblings, and no other family members would step up to care for her.

Cartel sat back down on the couch. "Wren, I know speaking about your mother is a touchy subject for you. Yet, I stand here as an evangelist who strives to think and do as Jesus would do. I am reminded in my spirit that the Bible speaks to honor our parents. We are to honor them no matter what. And yes, even when we disagree with their decisions. On top of that, I yearn so badly for my mother and father."

"Here you go with all that stuff. Killing the vibe of my award night." Wren snapped.

"Well, it needs to because your mother Sharon is still alive. She served a 12-year sentence and had a life as bad as your messed-up childhood. Every time she walks into my hair salon, she inquiries about you. I believe it would allow you to love if you forgave her."

"Do you want to know what I think?" Wren smirked, getting up from her chair. "If she wanted to be in my life, she would have stayed around. Instead, she decided to ride for a man, who turned out NOT to be our father. What mother would take a drug case for a man and leave her children? Only a woman who loved her man more than her children."

"Now, that is not fair, Wren! You think she loved your dad more than Steven and you?"

"All I know is that I was twelve years old, Cartel! I had to step up and be a parent to my seven-year-old brother. It has been twenty-six years, and I do not want to discuss her mistake tonight. I want to enjoy the remainder of the night in peace."

"You are right. My apology! Let us toast to this award, this blessing of many more." Cartel got up and walked over to Wren with her glass of wine.

Wren looked over at her trophy sitting on her fireplace mantel. She smiled from ear to ear. She knew Cartel's thoughts were valid regarding her mother, but she was not ready. "Um, one question. Should we be toasting with wine?" Wren asked. "I thought people toast with champagne?"

"Come on now, Wren, we've always set our standards."

"Now that is true, explaining why I have a lazy boy chair sitting in my sunroom. Most people would think it is out of line because they decorate with patio furniture. Now let us toast to that!" In laughter, they toasted.

"I am so glad that you're home, Wren."

"It is good to be back at home, my friend." Wren tried hard not to look at the trophy again, but it embellished challenging work and dedication. At 38 years of age, she was no longer a lost little girl. Today, Wren stood as a successful Black woman and an award-winning celebrity fashion designer living her dream. She had a million dollars net worth and finally found her way.

The following day the ladies decided to meet up for brunch at one of their favorite spots to eat, Chicago's Home of Chicken and Waffles. Wren was excited to be home. Los Angeles had places to eat, but nothing came close to the food at home. The ladies settled into their seats. The restaurant was full of customers as the norm. Chicagoans knew where to find great food.

"So, Ms. Cartel, how is the amazing marriage going?" Wren started the conversation.

"Whelp, we just celebrated our fifth anniversary. That said, I would say great." Cartel said, wiggling around in her chair, attempting to find comfort.

"That is impressive! When will you have a baby?" Wren then asked, sipping from a glass of water on the table.

"We have been trying Wren, and it is just not happening. At times, I attempt to find reasons for blame. Believing it is because we work long hours or missed the mark. With George being a barber and myself being an outreach street evangelist and hairstylist, our schedules are hectic. I spend my entire day and late evenings on the streets, witnessing or inside the salon. However, George is free to do whatever once he finishes cutting hair for the day. I am starting to believe what happened in the past is the cause of my miscarriages."

Wren's eyes widened, nodding her head in disbelief. She had no idea Cartel was still struggling with the horrible foster care experience. "No, you two might be missing ovulation. Have you tried fertility treatments?" Wren asked, struggling to find the right words to say. She knew nothing about the topic and that some women battled with ovulation and others could not have children. Wren did not want to believe her friend, Cartel, could not get pregnant or carry a baby to full-term. She also wondered why Cartel never shared her pain with her husband. It was like having a secret and not knowing who or what you married.

"You know George; he is not for the unnecessary efforts and medication risks. He feels if it is God's will, it will happen."

"God, huh" Wren shrugged her shoulders and mumbled. *This God stuff is getting ridiculous. She should know by now there is no God, but whatever!* Wren laughed. "Yeah, okay, but you are 37 now. Unless he does not want children, he should change his mind fast."

"Agreed." Cartel replied, ignoring Wren's ill feelings toward God. It was evident that Wren was an Atheist; she did not believe in God. Having a best friend as an Atheist made it difficult for Cartel. "Wren, when will you marry and have children?"

"Well, first, I will never marry because men do not take marriage vows seriously. Look at Daniel; my so-called father divorced my mother almost ninety days into her sentence. He met that light-skinned, redhead chico stick and was gone with the wind. I knew she did not like my brother and me from day one. She is the person who convinced Daniel to DNA test us. I am good on the marriage stuff."

The server came by and took their orders. After completing their food order, a handsome-looking, brown-skinned, muscle tone gentlemen walked over to their table. "Wren Davidson! I saw your emotional acceptance speech last night. I just came over to say congratulations!"

"Thank you, yes, it has been quite a journey for me, but I am grateful." Wren smiled at him.

"Well, keep making us proud; not often we get noticed. I will let you ladies continue. Have a blessed day!"

"Okay, sis! Somebody is getting celebrity-style exposure in this place. See, he could be your potential husband. You must stop living with limitations. Your parent's mistakes are not your destiny." Cartel explained.

"You do realize my disbelief in that fairy tale stuff, right? There is no such thing as forever love. People come and go for many reasons. Lucky for me, my childhood exposed that truth early in life. I am good over here."

Cartel shrugged her shoulders at Wren. "You are not good, but I will continue to pray for you."

"Cartel, I wish you would stop worshipping a fairytale God. He is not up there, honey! If there were a loving God, he would not have allowed my brother and me to grow up without parents. He would not have allowed for you to grow up parentless either."

If there were one thing Cartel could change about Wren, it would be her stiffened heart. Her continuous battle with not allowing anyone to get close to her. And the fact that she blamed God for all hardships was a bit much. Cartel had hoped by now she was past this state of mind. Her mother sold drugs too. Although their mothers made poor choices, they were still their mothers.

Exchanging smiles during silence was best. Cartel exhaled. They knew each other all too well not to tick each other off. "I am over it, Wren; please change the subject!"

"Cartel, I am fine. My decisions are reasonable," Wren discerned her friend's unhappy spirit. She realized her reluctance to date and her rejection of God annoyed Cartel. Partaking in silence for a minute or two longer drove Wren crazy. She had to break the silence. "Cartel, is it that serious about my opposition to date or get married? Come on; we were having a wonderful time catching up here. Smile a little."

Cartel responded, "It bothers me, Wren. I understand that your father was wrong for promising his relationship with you would not change. He was very uncaring to promise that and leave. Yet, all men are not equal. You have hardened your heart towards men in general. If you keep this up, you will become a lonely old soul."

"Now, that was good. I like the thought of being a lonely old soul. At least it cannot get wounded. And here comes our food. Right on time!" Wren said, escaping the conversation. The server placed their food on the table.

Without saying grace, Wren immediately started munching away at her food.

"Somebody is hungry and ungrateful to God. I will say grace for the both of us." Cartel began to pray silently over their food.

"Yeah, yes, yeah. Oh, and I must add that I failed to mention I met Oscar-winning actor Casanova Bryant. He was at the CFDA awards in New York the night of filming the show. He asked me to go to breakfast the next morning; we went to breakfast and dinner. We still talk on the phone every day. He is a cool person."

"That is good news. How long has this been going on?" Cartel inquired, taking a bite of her waffle.

"Well, as you know, filming for the awards was several weeks ago. I was surprised to learn he does not have children."

Cartel shrugged her shoulders. Casanova was not the first man Wren met in her lifetime. The issue was not attracting men; it was upholding their interests.

Dating a man long enough to establish a relationship is where she failed.

What has gotten into you?" Wren could sense the disconnect. She wondered if the distance had caused their friendship to fade. Wren could not recall Cartel being so dull.

Shaking her head back and forth, reluctant to express her concerns, but did anyway. "Why even waste this man's time? Your heart is full of pain. It would take a clever man to soothe those wounds. My prayer is that a man is out there up for the challenge. I sure hope Mr. Casanova has great intentions. Lord knows you do not need an opportunist invading your thoughts and heart with lies. Selfish intentions would take you over the edge."

"Whatever happened to make you stronger? When negative things happen, it is to make you stronger. That was how we interpreted bad experiences, remember? Plus, Casanova does not fit into the opportunist equation. His acting career in television and movies makes his resume and finances longer than long. And did I mention he is finer than fine?"

Cartel giggled. "Now, that is for sure! Casanova is one of the sexist and wealthiest actors in the spotlight. He is in the same lineup with Morris Chestnut and Denzel Washington."

The ladies finished their meals and ended their reunion embracing in hugs. They were glad to be back in each other's company.

Discussions over the phone once per week just were not enough. Being amid company was good for the soul. Cartel was ecstatic that Wren had returned home to Chicago. She prayed that this transition would not demise Wren's fashion career yet open more doors of opportunity.

Casanova Bryant returned home to Chicagoland after being on the road for approximately eight months. He had just finished filming in New York and was ready to surround himself with family and close friends.

A celebration dinner was underway inside his Hinsdale, Illinois, five-bedroom home. Not surprised by the usual festivity, he toasted champagne with his father.

As the only child, he grew up in an upscale lifestyle fit for royalty. A lifestyle most people only imagined. Groomed from a young boy, a queen should serve her King. His father, Gregory Bryant, the CEO of a computer software company. His mother, Anna Bryant, the CEO and President of a wealth management company. He lived in a white neighborhood and attended schools with few children of color. His childhood was still quite normal. It was rich and full of love.

His mother catered to his father's every need while maintaining a work-life balance. She still found time to stay abreast of Casanova's life, which carried into his adult life. Many women have come and gone on her watch, attributing to some discovery the fit was unequally yoked.

Today was a new day in Casanova's life. The Oscars and fame were nothing compared to the joy he found in Wren Davidson. He looked forward to their daily talks, and in his mind, his future had a place for her.

"My son, taking in Oscar awards now! I am sure you anticipated a victory dinner." His father complimented him after not seeing him in months.

Casanova smirked and elbowed his old man. Casanova and his father shared a tight bond. His father was always straightforward and never sugar-coated anything. He was very down-to-earth and never glorified wealth. "Pops, I met this woman while I was in New York. She is a fashion designer, a black one at that. Never in my life has a woman caught my attention on an attractive and intelligent level as she did. If she stays this way, I am going to marry her. I know I will."

"She must be something because I was starting to worry about you, man. You are forty years old with no children. I was beginning to think we went wrong with you." His father teased.

Suddenly, a woman approached. A beautiful Black woman with caramel color skin stood before him. She smiled extremely hard with all her white teeth showing. Casanova stared her up and down. Her petite body tone, professionally polished red nails, and medium-length chestnut brown hair were everything. Dressed in an all-black dress added elegance and a new touch of class to her attire.

"Are you surprised?" she questioned. Her eyes were seductive, her voice soft-spoken. Casanova was indeed attracted to her. Refusing to blink his eyes, he wanted to capture every detail of her essence.

"Minnie Trading!" Casanova greeted with a super smile, "The one and only daughter and sister of the Trading's law group attorneys!" Casanova admired this woman for years but somehow could never obtain her attention. He could not believe she stood before him and inside his living room. It became logical that she had received the news of his recent award. Her character defined a snobbish woman who was careful not to depreciate her reputation for the likes of the lower class. To gain her attention, a man of her standards had to be great in the title and uphold respect in the community.

"I got invited over by your mother. I am honored to be here to celebrate your success this evening. Congratulations to you, job well done!" she smiled.

Casanova's smile began to fade. *My mother invited her over.* A woman like Minnie, her standards made him unsure of her motive. Her overconfident smile gave way, which suddenly aggravated him. She could never be his type. They originated from two different planets and shared almost nothing in common. "Why did you accept my mother's invitation?" he asked out of curiosity.

"Do not be silly, Cass! I think we both know why I accepted the invite."

"I did not mean to be silly. Back in the day, I could not buy your attention. So, tell me, what is different today? What did I do to earn your devotion?"

Surprised by his unfriendliness, she displayed the nastiest facial expression. "You are just as I thought. A difficult breed is why I never paid you any attention. I could never," she added, walking away.

Casanova was suspicious of women who only recognized one's achievements but not their inner being. He knew that since his career heightened to national attention, he was now a huge factor, according to her standards.

"That was a little rude, Cass," His father stood embarrassed. "She comes from a family of very reputable Black millionaire attorneys. One of Chicago's finest. Why discredit her in such a way? We might need to pull some of those strings in the future."

"Her family is successful, but what has she done to contribute to her family's success?

Besides, I know her kind. I do not want a woman who only recognizes my success. I want one who recognizes my heart. If I lost every dollar I have earned tomorrow, she would be first to leave me."

"I understand that. And, I will not argue your point," sharing another toast. "But Minnie is a paralegal for the group, and you could have turned her away in a respectful mannerism, son, dang!

"Dad, I only asked the woman a question. She felt the discernment and made a way of escape. I had nothing to do with that."

"Yeah, you might be right." His father shrugged.

"Now, about Wren Davidson. Pops! This woman is everything; attractive, successful, no children, intelligent. Just God sent! She is from the Chicago area and just moved back home. She just won her first designer award."

"So, are you planning to spend time with her while home and not filming?"

"Yes, but I am only home for two months, then I am back on the road filming again. I must call Wren up to see what is on her calendar. If all goes well, I might get an opportunity to bring her to meet you and mom."

"Well, make sure she is who you want before bringing her to your mother. Your mother is no easy win. With that, you might need to prepare Wren for the mother exam. She is one tough person, especially regarding you.

"That is true." Casanova agreed. He looked across the room at his mother, Anna. She was conversing with Minnie Trading. Casanova wondered how involved his mother had been with Minnie lately. Wren's position got more complicated if his mother and Minnie had grown close while he was on the road. His eyes met with his mom. If the impact of her stare could stab like a knife, it would be fatal.

Standing unsure of her motives, he shrugged his shoulder. He redirected his attention back toward his father. Thoughts of Wren recollected in his mind. Thrilled that he finally found a woman who challenged his mental, he was glad to have shared the news with his father.

"Casanova, your mother, is walking in this direction. Her face alerts me that she is not happy with something. All I ask is that you not let her ruin this evening. Stand your ground in a respectful tone." His father warned, taking another glass of champagne from a server passing by.

"Who is she? Casanova!" his mother approached. It was clear that Minnie Trading was Anna's preferred choice. She knew Casanova had admired her, and bringing them together this evening should have been the celebration's highlight. She thought, anyway.

"What in the devil is going on around here?" he asked, "Since when did you become the Trading law group spoke person, bestie?

"You have admired her for years, Casanova. You have earned her attention and blew it for what purpose?"

He opted out of the truth. "I am a little tired and would like to relax a bit. Everyone is welcome to stay and continue celebrating; I will dismiss myself."

"Casanova, you are an adult. I cannot make you view things the way I do, but I would still like to know who has your heart." she pressed.

Casanova found himself still reluctant to express his disinterest in Minnie to his mother. The energy to explain his reasons was not there, nor did he feel obligated. He respected his mother's efforts to ignite the flame, but Minnie was no longer the apple of his eye. It was time Anna stayed in her place and allowed him to find his own good thing.

"Why would you keep her a secret, Cass?" his mother, now annoyed by how Casanova continued to skirt around the requested information.

"Oh, she is not a secret." He responded. "I am not ecstatic about Minnie Trading's presence, is what you must understand. If that disappoints you, I am sorry. According to you, every woman has not been virtuous enough for one reason or another. I have realized that I cannot allow you to help find my wife."

"Boy, you better watch your tone," Anna responded. She stepped closer to his face.

"Anna, hear the words from this man, who is not a little boy. Let him grow up and manage his adult affairs." Gregory interrupted. Anna gawked at her husband. In disbelief, he would silence her when they both should be concerned about their son's involvement. Casanova's decisions impacted their family's throne. Since Anna would not dare overstep Gregory's authority, she furiously silenced herself.

Anna came from one of the poorest neighborhoods in Chicago, Fuller Park. She worked hard through college and built her business from scratch. When she met her husband, Gregory, it was not long before the two discovered a force not to be messed over. However, they often bumped heads because Anna had to learn to be submissive and lay down the leader in her. Gregory's mother, Rose Anne, believed a woman should submit to her husband. She grew fond of Anna's resentment and taught her to become a virtuous woman.

"I will give you an answer to appease your desire, mother. Her name is Wren Davidson!"

"You have got to be kidding me. That overnight success! No way! She is here today and gone tomorrow. Fashion designers have temporary limelight. Get over it already!" Anna snapped.

"Minnie has nothing but inheritance." Casanova reminded.

"A lifetime of inheritance, Casanova. Do not belittle your worth. You have my future grandchildren to think about. What is Wren native? Hood? The way she spoke during that acceptance speech the other night, slang was all I heard. She needs a lot of fine-tuning. Did you hear that girl's journey? Her childhood was a nightmare. And do you want to bring that into this family? She is hood and not welcomed in this family."

"Really? Did you label that woman a hood chick? Do you not recall your upbringing? How easy we forget." Casanova rebuttal. He was not into discrediting people, especially when not given a fair chance."

"She is known for her creative attire. Nothing more! What is she like, Casanova? When did you find so much time to invest in her anyway? What are her family values, and most importantly, her religion?"

Casanova grew silent. He had no desire to explain what value he found in Wren to his mother. He recognized his mother's antics to dig and dig for more information to make a valid point; he was not about to play the game.

"Cass, I did ask you a question. What is so great about her?"

Fighting to ignore her offensive comments about Wren, he gazed upward towards the vaulted ceiling. His mind rummaged for ways to escape the unpleasant conversation. *Exiting the kitchen would cause her to follow. When did she become so arrogant? The fact that she had forgotten she was a product of Chicago's poorest neighborhoods.* At times, it was tough to receive her altered ego.

Holding back uncomfortable feelings, Anna wanted to recollect a calm approach. The goal was to change his mindset, not aggravate him. His silence made it difficult to determine his angle. The thought of Wren's presence around her son was so nerve-racking.

Anna knew how it felt to struggle financially in life, so she and her husband worked hard to ensure their son would not endure those hardships. She was confident that the joining of Minnie and him would be beneficial. They were both from wealthy families who ensured that her grandchildren would embark upon an affluent lifestyle. Wren Davidson was not idealistic, and Anna was determined to prove this to Casanova.

A text message populated across Casanova's cellular device. It read, *"Just thinking of you, and how it would be great to see you soon."* It was Wren. His mouth, now with a widened grin. Without hesitation, he responded, *dinner? Tomorrow at 7 pm?"* He awaited her response. A dinner date with her tomorrow evening was just what he desired. Her irresistible challenge and power spellbound him.

Anna stood curious about the message content. "Was that her?" she asked, "Do you want to give up everything? After living and maintaining a wealthy and peaceful lifestyle, you go out there and decide to choose a woman of her standard. A messy, low-class, and definite overnight celebrity. Cass?"

"Anna, I am going to say this just one more time. Our son is not a child. We are not usually the ones that handle choosing his mate. God gives him the discernment in choosing the wife he has for him. I do not want to repeat myself!" Gregory told her.

"So, Gregory, you are okay with our son's decision to date this hood girl?" Anna asked, turning to face him.

"Anna, you heard what I said. Our son is forty years old. I mean, he did mention that. Also, any woman he so chooses is his choice, and we will respect it. Enough about this already. He is just dating her; he didn't say he was marrying her tomorrow."

"And to add to that, I can make my own decisions. You are my father's rib. Your vow to God was to honor, love, and be my father's backbone. I am to find my queen that will do the same. My rib!"

Anna turned to Casanova once again. It was not that she had any real issues with Wren; the unknown concerned her. Anna recognized Wren Davidson's work from afar. She owned a few of her elegant after-five gowns. Yet Wren's sudden rise to fame was too new to be successful. Fly by night was more fitting. Or, here today, and gone tomorrow. Meaning, so will her money.

With Casanova's ten years of personal wealth and the inheritance he would acquire from them, she desired a great and wealthy mate. She decided to halt her opinions and hoped Casanova would never connect to Wren. Removing herself from the conversation, she returned to the other side of the room to entertain guests.

Casanova exhaled. He was relieved that the conversation had ended and could depart to his living quarters. Lying across his bed in deep thought, he muttered a short vow not to let Anna hinder his likeness of Wren. After just two dates, Wren appeared different. Something was challenging about her. He just needed to discover what it was that mesmerized him. The chase was appealing to him, and nothing mattered more. His cellphone vibrated. Wren had accepted his dinner invitation. With that, his night was complete.

The next evening Wren and Casanova arrived in separate cars at one of Chicago's downtown fine dining restaurants overlooking the city skyline. Wren came dressed in a navy-blue short-length fitted dress. Her red bottom shoes and matching red purse made her stand out in the crowd. Wren Davidson was by far the best-looking dark-skinned woman Casanova had ever seen. He helped her into her seat, delighted to be dining with her.

She quickly observed Casanova's attire and shoes as he took his seat. She nodded her head and giggled. Something about his tan pants with a white polo shirt and Gucci horsebit slippers made her laugh. As a stylist, he could use her help with coordinating fits. Well, at least his feet are lotioned.

The server introduced himself and started them off with water and an order of warm bread. The two ordered a shareable along with two glasses of red wine. Casanova glanced at Wren as she studied the menu. This evening, she was quieter than on their first two dates; he wondered if something was troubling her. "May I share something with you?" he asked.

"Sure, what's up?" she looked up and waited for his response.

"I stayed up late last night thinking about you for some reason. Are you part Indigenous person in descent? You are lovely, and that long wavy grade of hair is flawless."

Not flattered by his compliments, she ignored them. She was unaware of any Indian traits or knew their connection in her family line. She barely knew her mother's side of the family, which hurt her slightly, and her father is unknown. *What if my birth father was an Indigenous person?* She thought for a moment. *What if Casanova is a cousin of mine?* She looked away, noticing a glass of water on the table. Quickly, she grabbed the glass and sipped it repeatedly. An uneasy feeling rushed over her.

"A bit nervous?" He asked. Watching as she repeatedly sipped the water. "Usually, a compliment is followed by gratitude."

"Oh, thank you for the hair compliment." She responded, still sipping the water.

"So, do you attend church?" he asked, trying to start some discussion.

"Sometimes. Do you?"

"Sometimes? He repeated. Could you elaborate a little more?"

"I do not attend church, dude. I do not believe in this God most people idolize."

"Dude?" He repeated. Now that was different from the first impression of her. The short-answered dialog and dude slang was sure to annoy him. Desperate to understand Wren, he approached the conversation from a different angle. "Is something wrong tonight?"

"No, I am good." She sipped the water once more.

Casanova nodded his head. His brain split between confused and more confused. The woman he had met the other morning was not the same woman sitting across the table from him. He detected irritation from her body language but still couldn't make the connection.

"Why are you just staring, man?" Wren turned her nose up at him. She wanted to say something to Casanova but struggled to proceed.

"Why are you here, Wren? I sense that you honestly don't want to be here with me. Why did you bother to text me?"

"Truthfully? Do you want to know?" she leaned in to respond.

"Tell me something. You are starting to make me think you are bipolar or something. Our breakfast and dinner date were amazing, we had a connection, but today, you are acting weird. I am about ready to leave, like right now."

Wren burst into laughter. She could tell Casanova was getting aggravated, and his toughness was cute. "Honestly, I texted you after having a lengthy conversation with my best friend. I was not feeling this date or any date with a man." She answered.

"Are you saying that you are into women?" Casanova asked as the server brought back their wine and appetizer. He placed it on the table.

"Dude, stop playing with me! My thing is, men put their best foot forward trying to impress a woman, and then months later -the real deal is exposed. Would you please not focus on impressing me? Just be cool, man, gangster cool. If something is supposed to be, let it happen naturally. Also, I can tell you are a mother's boy, man!"

"Is gangster cool?" Casanova was not impressed by her comments. The woman he raved about to his parents was an undercover thug. He sat quietly, not sure of how to respond. Although he liked her idea of letting things happen as they should, he was unsure if he could accept slang and a gangster love type of woman. He hoped she was using those words lightly and that this was not the real deal. "Where are you from?" He was hoping to discover the root cause of this gangster demeanor.

"I am from the south side of Chicago. Where are you from?"

"I grew up in Hinsdale, not too far from Chicago. So really? Are you into the thug gangster type of men?" Casanova teased, hoping she would say no, and that she would also find his comment humorous.

"Nope. A hardworking type of man. I was not born with a silver spoon in my mouth as you were, but I learned the importance of a college education incredibly early in life. Especially when you are Black in America, we must have all our ducks in a row to move up any ladder of success."

Whelp, at least her response was intelligent, he thought. As his mother pointed out, Wren is a wise woman with a hood demeanor. Relived she could speak proper English if needed, her splash of slang might be tolerable. He discerned Wren as strong-minded and unwavering, and her journey could unveil a phenomenal woman. He wanted so badly to believe that anyway. He thought about his mother; if ever given the satisfaction that she was right about Wren, he would never hear the end of it. "So, how did you feel about me pulling out your chair and opening the car door for you?" Casanova threw out more questions.

"Honestly, I can open and close my door. Those gestures are meaningless to me. I thought you were a hopeless romantic type of guy. You cannot flatter me with those gestures. I am down to earth. Let us eat, drink beers, pass gas, and laugh."

"Drink beers and pass gas? You are kidding, right?" he asked, now disgusted. This chick was serious, Casanova gathered. He shook his head. His appetite now dissolved from thinking too hard about the situation. "What made you this way? Why are you so hard-core and just this man type of chick? And where was she at in New York?"

Puzzled, she asked, "What do you mean? How am I made? Either I am a woman or a man, Casanova. I cannot be both!"

In today's world, you can be anything you want. Casanova thought to himself. He withdrew his response. The last thing he needed was to start an argument in an upscale restaurant with a hood chick.

The server returned to place their order. Wren ordered her food and waited for him to place an order. "Are you going to order?"

"I am not even hungry, sweetheart. Sir, I will take another glass of red wine. I am good." He instructed, motioning for the server to speed things along.

"Do I make you nervous?" Wren then asked, now concerned about his actions.

Nervous would be considered an understatement. Casanova thought. He was borderline done with this date and Wren altogether. His thoughts continued. *She must have experienced a traumatic episode to act out and develop this hard-core type of mannerism.* He valued her realness but despised her negativity toward chivalry. He finally answered her. "No, I am not nervous at all."

"Dude, do not live so serious, alright. Live a little! Mother's boy!"

"What does that mean?" Casanova questioned.

"Listen, man; you might have gathered that I am focused on success, not a relationship. Men have not been genuine in my world. Their intentions have been selfish, and I am not feeling any man. Got it?"

"No, I do not get it. I am not men; I am a man as in my person. What others have done has nothing to do with me. I also do not understand why you are telling me all of this. Of course, I want to get to know you, but I do not understand your approach. Why are you carrying baggage around? I thought you were a confident lady up until this point. Who are you? "

"Baggage? What gives you that impression? Wait! I am good with that term. Casanova Bryant, I am okay with carrying baggage. I have every right to carry around baggage. You have no idea what I have experienced in life, but I will tell you this much, it helps me identify men with boyish intentions. The baggage you claim I am carrying has equipped me to care less!" her voice sharpened. Her eyes widened.

Casanova sensed frustration and backed off a bit. She was completely different today than she was the other day. *How could she switch up like that?* He scratched his head. Yet still, he wanted to know more. He hoped to understand her hardness. "Did you grow up with a father in your life? Like seriously, what is wrong with you? Why do you have so much attitude?" Casanova continued to dig.

"Casanova, why do you ask such stupid questions, man? What difference does it make if my father was present or not? I had an interest in you until I learned something about you yesterday. Already, you are implying that I am fatherless, and due to that, I am a misguided Black woman." She rose from the table, "This is why I do not date; too much of a headache. Dealing with men raises my blood pressure. Understand that you are not my type. I cannot relate to men who allow their mother to dictate their life." She left the restaurant.

Casanova noted that mentioning her father lit the flame. Her father's presence or non-presence was the root of her hard-core act. He ignored being a mother's boy or man. He placed four hundred dollars cash on the table to pay for Wren's meal, which she never received and followed her out of the restaurant.

"Are you this messed up?" he continued to jab at her, catching up with her. His thoughts were to press the issue longer. He wanted her to get whatever it was out and in the open. He was up for the challenge. And besides, he could hear his mother's words, and he refused to lose to her.

"Let me explain something to you. When I texted you yesterday evening, I had just finished listening to your conversation with your mother or some woman acting like a mother or boss. I heard her inquire about my success. You & I have nothing in common. That woman sounded like a Black uncle Tom, well she's a woman so, Aunt Tomika. It is great that she is successful, but to declass her own. That is a bit ridiculous! I worked too hard to get where I am, and I will never let your type make me feel like I have not accomplished much."

Probing for a comeback, he had none. Upset that Wren had heard any of that. Casanova recognized a sudden change in her demeanor but never thought it resulted from his carelessness. *Dang! My phone auto-dialed her. I exposed her to my mother's messiness.* He felt terrible that Wren uncovered all that information. He was not sure if he should hold her or let her vent. "Listen, Wren…" he began.

"Dude, roll with that! Could you be honest with that woman? I bet she is your mother, huh? Can you tell her that I am from the south side of Chicago? Ready to face her and discuss my truth? No, because she already has standards for your ideal mate."

Casanova remained calm and wordless. *Answering her would ruin any chance he had with her.* His mother was like a warden when it came to him. She would never accept Wren for whom she was if he told her the truth. *This girl does not add up to my parent's expectations. I cannot bring her home to my parents. Not like this anyway.*

"Just like I thought. You cannot even answer. Men are never genuine at heart. You all are selfish creatures. You began to develop a strong likeness for me, Casanova, but your feelings have changed because of my origin. Nope, let me rephrase that. I meant; that your selfish pride will not allow you to date me. I am on your level, but not your parent's level or whomever that person was in the background. I need a few more accolades and more dollars to achieve a man of your standards. My bad, I meant the approval of your parents because you like me, and you know you do."

"That is true. I do like you. Well, I like the woman I met in New York."

"This is crazy, having to prove yourself to your people? Your parents are Black, correct Casanova? If so, I am not sure where that lady fell off, but brown/tan will always be her skin color. The roots will always be there. I will never understand why our people are against each other on every level. This world is nothing without us, and we are nothing without each other."

Contemplating between leaving and staying, he harked on his feelings. He recalled how he had felt in the eyes of Minnie Trading. He was never Minnie's type until he had reached another level of success or another tax bracket. Wren was right; judging a book by its cover was not cool. That is what he longed for – a woman to love his heart and not his money. "Wren, I apologize, sweetheart, for my mother's unkind words."

"Dude, I am not feeling that weak apology. You are a mother's boy! I can gather she is a piece of work. You battled back and forth in thought, debating riding off and leaving me alone or staying, correct? I could read your thoughts. I do not want you having to defend me to your peeps or anyone. I am good with waiting for the one that is for me. He and his family would embrace me without any explanations."

"Wren, I am never judging you. I could care less about your past. We might come from distinct parts of Illinois, but that does not mean anything. Also, my mother does not define who I am and what is best for me. I am a man, not a child. She will be fine in time. Do you think we could start over?"

"It is cool. I do not think we will develop into anything more than a few dates anyway. I am from the hood! I lived in foster homes for most of my life. My parents left me to raise my younger brother on my lonesome. Do you still want to know me? Well, know that I stripped to pay for my brother and my college education. I am not proud of it, but we made it. Still want to get to know me now?"

"When you say strip, do you mean naked or partial? I would not be honest if I function as if that does not matter."

"Now, what I will not do, is apologize for my hardships or childhood. Either you can take me as I am or move forward; no loss here."

"Does that mean yes; you agree to start over?" He ignored Wren's attempt to validate her hoodism. He was genuinely hoping for a fresh start. She stripped for a living bothered him because he was unsure if the stripping involved after sets with several men, but he was still willing to start over. "Are you willing to go out with me again?"

"If you want, then sure" she grinned at him. She was relieved that he was still up for the challenge, especially after announcing that she was a stripper. Wren had never expressed her hardships to any man outside her brother Steve. Although she did strip for a living at one point, she had never had sex before. She was still a virgin and scared of being hurt by men. "You're a weird dude." She laughed.

"I can be a little weird and different at times. I must agree." He reached for her hand. She moved away from him.

Casanova felt extremely bad that Wren heard such insulting comments over the phone. Any friendship or relationship should not start with negative family involvement; it should never happen in any relationship, period. However, the message was clear to him. Wren had never acquired true love. He reached for her hand again. He was optimistic about helping restore her soul if only she would allow him.

Wren pushed his hand back again. She was not sure why he continued to reach for her hand. After several gestures from Casanova, she followed suit and accepted his hand. He pulled her close to him, holding her in his arms. He felt sympathy and a strong attraction. If genuine love was all she needed, he was sure to provide. They walked the nearby lakefront; the weather was warm and welcomed the beautiful view of the Chicago skyline. Many spectators were enjoying the warm weather by walking alongside the lakefront.

"You are a tough sister but extremely beautiful," He complimented. "Although I can feel so much hesitation from you, I know you are enjoying this."

Wren was taken back by Casanova's smooth response. His words were thoughtful, which reminded her of Cartel. She had expected to hear, "*You are crazy, stuck up, or misguided!*" But Casanova was a smooth operator. His effort to remain at her side was a good thing. It was awkward to let a man hold her. Yet to her surprise, it did feel good.

"One more question," he added, "and this might make you angry again, but I am willing to fight for an answer. Were you serious about not attending church regularly?"

"Yes, Casanova. I am not sure about this God Spirit. My childhood would not have been bad if there were a God. A loving God would not allow children to endure so much pain. If there is a God, like most men, he is selfish to allow my brother and me to go through."

He waited for her to say more, not expecting to hear such derogatory comments toward God. For a moment, he wondered if his mother's opinions were valid. *Is this job too big for him? Or is this woman just a diamond in the ruff?* Immediately he erased the negative thoughts and chose to believe the positive. His parents did not recognize he, too, struggled with believing in God at times. He believed in a higher power but was not sure if the higher power was from the same God his parents honored.

"I am sorry you endured such hardship during your childhood. Have you ever thought that God allowed you to endure those hardships to reach back and help others survive or heal? Why were you in foster homes to begin with?" he asked.

"Not so soon, man. I cannot spill out all my business. I mean, you appear great and all, but over time. Just be glad I gave you this much." She replied, holding up a pinched finger.

"I can respect that answer, and it is fair."

"Do you attend church faithfully?" she asked.

"Not as much as I should, but I believe in God."

"And I bet you give God glory for your hard work and achievements, too, huh? The work you put in to win awards and establish a lavish lifestyle."

"I do give God the glory. I would not be here if it were not for God's providing. He awarded me the gift of acting and entertaining the world. It is him that protects me along the way. In anything I star in, I always honor God in a statement or two. I write that into any role I take, and so far, it is respected regardless of the movie storyline or content. When I interview, I give major props to the Highest because I want people to understand that I can do nothing without him."

Wren laughed aloud. She found those statements delusional. *"How could one glorify someone they had never seen? That is so stupid and unrealistic."*

Casanova pulled away from her. "You are serious, huh?"

"I am. I am so serious. My girl Cartel labeled me an Atheist." She responded.

Casanova refused to believe she was an Atheist, as scary as that sounds. Instead, he focused on her unique attributes. He hoped that she would allow him the chance to push away those other heavy barricades. Wren is the true definition of a diamond in the ruff. Her dislike of God would soon change; he was sure of it.

"Casanova, it is getting pretty late, so I better get home," Wren recommended.

He pulled her close to him again. He needed just a few more minutes with her. Their first date in Illinois was quite different from New York. Casanova learned a new thing about Black women. He did not think Black women, as fine as she, came wrapped in so much pain. Why would a man be crazy enough to abuse her type? "Will I see you again?" he asked.

"Do you want to see me again? I mean, after all this mess tonight?"

"What mess? I did not notice a thing." He smiled, releasing her from his arms. "But on a serious note, there is some growing to do. Our backgrounds are different, which might cause us not to understand each other at times. Of course, if we have something solid, we must build upon it."

"Thank you for a great evening, Cass."

"Cass? Giving me nicknames already? Wren, you did not answer my question. When will I see you again?"

"We will figure something out. Right now, I need to get back to my hood."

"Wren? You do not still live on the Southside, do you? Never mind, do not answer that. Come on, let me walk you to your car."

"No, I do not live on the Southside anymore. I moved to Naperville. And thank you, Casanova, for a great night. I appreciate your kindness." She added, getting in her car.

Chapter Two: Married Now (six months later)

It was a quarter after 3 pm on Saturday. Wren stood inside an Alii suite shared with Casanova in the beautiful and romantic Royal Hawaiian. She just made a decision that could impact her future negatively or positively. Rethinking her actions, she paced across a light beige rug perfectly centered on the floor. In their King's size bed, Casanova squirmed to find comfort. Wren observed, hoping not to wake him from his nap.

Last night was beautiful. A perfect Friday night to marry in Honolulu, HI. Although marriage was not in her plans, the oceanfront atmosphere made it right. She loved Casanova, which was an accomplishment. However, marriage is a legally binding contract that should never get signed without thought. She stumbled across the floor, hitting her foot against an ottoman. She glanced at Casanova once more, who finally rested peacefully. She thought about their family and friends back home, who would have different opinions and feelings concerning their elopement.

Cartel would feel betrayed because the two never kept life-changing secrets from each other. Steven would want her to nullify the union until he approves of Casanova. The worst acceptance of this news would be Casanova's mother, Anna. Wren rolled her eyes at the thought of her. That pain in the butt would take a knife to her throat to permanently eliminate her from Casanova's life.

Although they were together for six months, Anna barely spoke to Wren. She recalled the day Casanova introduced her to his parents. They had been dating for about two months when he drove her out to their home. Anna did not shake her hand; instead, she asked many questions. However, his father, Gregory, was more than friendly. He was an absolute gentleman who greeted her with open arms. When that evening ended, Anna and Wren left on terms of mutual respect for Casanova. That meant an agreement to be cordial.

Another reason Wren battled with her decision was Casanova's chameleon spirit. In front of family or friends, he was the perfect gentleman. He blended and appeared to be a great man of faith with love and respect for her. Behind closed doors is where the exposed characters' true colors became known. Casanova was constantly correcting her speech, coaching her on what to say and when to say it. Her wardrobe had to be approved by him, especially before entertaining guests. It is like having a checklist of an ideal woman and how she should act, think, and speak. Anytime she defended herself, he became angry. There had been three occasions where their arguments became physical. *How did I commit to this lifestyle?*

She recalled the third occasion Casanova introduced the rod of correction, striking her with a belt as if she were a child. Unsure of his motives, she wrestled and fought to defend herself from Casanova. Wren did not know what a rod of correction was until he explained it in biblical terms. He implied the rod was a missing critical piece of her childhood. He encouraged her to trust and accept his authority as correction would only help her become a better woman.

Wren, who knew right from wrong, stood confused. *So, how did I end up here, married to the abuser?*

Wren made her way over to the coffee maker to brew a drink. Still tired from last night and had not slept since they became one. She searched through the tea and coffee selection she had bought earlier. A nearby hairbrush fell onto the floor, causing Casanova to move around the bed. Casanova was one of the lightest sleepers ever known. The smallest pin drop could wake him.

"Babe, are you okay?" Casanova looked up at her.

"Of course, I am just brewing a cup of coffee. I cannot fall asleep, so I got up." She answered.

Casanova sat up on the bed. He studied Wren for a moment. Casanova knew that Wren could not sleep very well if she were worried or nervous about something. He reflected on the many hurdles he had to help her overcome. "Mrs. Wren Davidson-Bryant! That name sounds good for you, woman!" he said. His goal was to ease her tremble.

She smiled at him. "I agree it does sound pretty good."

"Okay, why aren't you sleeping next to me?"

She smiled again while stirring cream and sugar in her coffee. Attempting to downplay the anxiety she felt to halt further conversation with Casanova. She did not want to discuss her thoughts that their marriage was a mistake. The timing was not the best, her thoughts were all over the place, and her words would come out wrong. Casanova found ways to make her feel bad about her beliefs in other unprepared attempts. He had her in a place of second-guessing herself most times. He was good at making her think she was delusional and stupid.

"Wren, I know you. Something is on your mind, and you should know by now that I will not rest until you speak on it." He propped a pillow against the backboard of the bed.

At that point, Wren knew he would never let up until she complied. She met him at his bedside, taking a seat on the floor, Indian style. "Casanova, out of all the women in the world. Why did you choose me?"

"Why not choose you?" he responded. "I mean, you are everything that I wanted in a wife. You are successful, beautiful, confident, a motivator, a boss, authentic woman. I wish you were God-fearing, but I pray that you will see God is God one day. Other than that, you are all I need."

"You say that, but your actions tell me you do not respect my thoughts or opinions. You get angry with me whenever I speak about uncomfortable situations involving your mother instead of listening. You downplay my gift in styling apparel, not allowing me to dress as I please. You and I have rehearsals advising me when and how to speak before entertaining family and friends. How does that line up with everything you need?"

Casanova rosed from the bed. He moved closer to her, throwing his arm around her shoulders. He could agree that she had been a work in progress, but he loved her. And he knew that she genuinely loved him.

Casanova hated that he had to put so much work into re-raising her at times. Wren got raised in the streets, which made things difficult at times. No one taught her how to be a lady or a wife.

Wren continued to speak her peace, "We barely dated for six months. The timing seems so premature. Did we give ourselves enough time to get to know each other? Will I add up to your ideal wife? Do you remember how hard it was for me to admit to falling in love with you? I have been an experience since you met me."

"Listen, all you must do is be a wife. Be the best wife that you can be, and never give up. We will make it." Casanova reassured.

"Are you sure about that? We have not discussed what you expect from marriage. I had no expectations because it was never part of my future. So, what do you see?

"Wren, marriage is a commitment, a promise made to you before God and never given up. My parents got married fifty years ago. I watched my mother juggle her career, raise me, help my father with his business, cook, clean, and keep home. She made it look easy. She had her hand in helping me find a wife because she believes if a woman knows her role as a wife, the marriage will last."

"My point exactly, I have no idea. Plus, who made up this role?"

Casanova laughed aloud and spoke. "God did!"

"God, huh? Well, no wonder I missed the memo. I do not allow fictional characters to advise me."

"Okay, today is where we draw the line on the disrespect of God. Just because you do not know much about him, I cannot allow you to continue to disrespect him. In marriage, the man is the head. As a man, God leads me. He is the King, and I am your King. And you, as my wife, will respect that."

"You know, I do not understand your God and this wife's role language. I would not say I like the way it sounds either. You are talking about being my head. It sounds so silly and strange to me. Like, what do I need you to lead or be ahead? I know how to survive in life. I understand how to tie my shoes, Casanova."

"Regarding that. I hold myself accountable for not putting this up before now. I am going to teach you the Bible. Every man wants that Proverbs 31 woman. Once you understand how a woman should behave, we will move ahead with everything else."

"Move ahead with what?" Wren asked, rising from the floor. At any moment, the quiet, mild-mannered conversation could switch up to a boxing match. She had to keep her guards up.

"One thing is sure; we will start our family this year. I want you pregnant tomorrow if I can make that happen. I am forty years old; I want all three of my children in the world in the next five years." Casanova rosed to join her.

Immediately Wren wanted out. Children never got discussed, and her opposing his wish is a recipe for disaster. She noted that Casanova never disagreed with her earlier comments about how he often scolded or corrected her. He would have instantly downplayed her mentions if she were indeed a good thing for him. It was not too late in annulling the union, which was best at the given moment. Wren took a seat on the bed. She started considering ways to break the news of her wanting out to him. She answered his demand for children. "How is it possible? I am at the peak of my career. I do not have time to mother children now."

"I know it is the peak season for you, but if you cannot bring forth our children and manage your career, then your job must come to a halt for the sake of our family. We need an heir to the throne." Casanova instructed, taking a seat on the bed next to her.

"Reason me?" Wren rose. "Here is what we did not discuss beforehand, Casanova. You cannot just set rules suddenly; I have a passion for art. This clothing industry is everything to me. It would be very selfish of you to halt this now for children. Unless you will sit at home and raise them while I continue to heighten my success."

"Wren! Seriously, how far does a celebrity apparel designer go? It is a limited success for most. When the next hot stylist arrives, they fade. You might have about five more years to shine before you dull. Moreover, I have this worked out for us. In ten more years, I will retire from acting myself. We will be in a place where all my investments and demanding work have paid off. We will live lavishly and continue to oversee our businesses while enjoying family life."

"Whose dream is that? It is not mine. Within a decade or less, I saw myself moving into other things like opening a design school. I see right now; we must cancel this thing because we disagree."

"We are not canceling or annulling anything, Wren; it is just a healthy disagreement. Stop running! I thought we were past those days. We agreed to a lifetime, so let us figure out how to make it work. At the end of the day, if your career does not line up with the family structure, babe, you will have to give it up. I am the protector and provider, ensuring we always have what we need and more. I do not need you worrying about all of that anymore. I know you had to care for Steven and you all your life and play protector, but I got us from here."

Back home in Chicago, Casanova and Wren decided that he would move into her home temporarily since his parents also accompanied him at his home. Together they would search for a new home in suburban Chicago to start their journey. Casanova was busy hanging his clothes in Wren's extra closet while she entertained Cartel in their living room.

"So, how did this marriage thing happen again?" Cartel asked, still in shock as they sat down on the loveseat. She knew Wren was not ready for marriage, nor was she prepared mentally to give up being the head of her castle.

"It just did. We chose not to wait and made it happen. Are you angry with me?"

Cartel did not think angry was the best word choice; it was more of a disappointment. Wren wanted to leave Casanova several times over the past six months. Without Cartel coaching her to stay in this thing with Casanova, there would be no marriage today. "No, I am not mad at you, just a little worried." Cartel answered.

"Do you want some wine?" Wren asked, getting up from the loveseat to pour up the drinks.

"Sure thing, just one glass, though, and very little, please."

Wren was ready to pour up some wine and pour out her heart to Cartel about the abuse she encountered with Casanova. She hoped to reason her thoughts and nullify the union before one of them got hurt. But first, Wren wanted Cartel to have an opportunity to update her on the loss of the baby. "So, what's this baby news?" she asked, back on the loveseat with Cartel.

"So, as you know, I have been pregnant in my mind at least three times now. The doctor gave us an update on my condition. He informed us that obesity might be contributing to ovulation. He went on to say my BMI is much over thirty, and this could be a factor. He thinks it may have played a part in the miscarriage too. However, you know my thoughts automatically converted to my childhood trauma."

"Well, what do you believe? I mean, I see thickness, but not obesity."

"I believe God, and I will have a baby if it is His will. If not, then I will not."

"You know, the way you worship this God person, he should give you the desires of your heart. Therefore, I cannot believe in such an idol. Why would he allow so much hardship and long-suffering? He knows you love him and honor him. Why can't he bless you with a baby?"

"Wren, it is not our will for our lives, but God's will. He might have a baby in store for George and me in the future; maybe the timing is not right. We must trust God even when we do not understand. If I cannot bear children, I will never blame God! He knows what is best regardless. My heart hurts because my husband's faith is weakening. I feel like he wants to give up on me at times."

"Now, that is a hard pill to swallow, friend. I hope he is not feeling that way. That might be the white girl part of you being all sensitive," Wren tried to make light. Being biracial (white & black), Cartel often got safely teased by Wren. "George loves you. He wants a baby, but he wants that baby with you." Wren sipped her wine, hoping what she spoke was the truth. If George walked out on Cartel, it would devastate her. Men are so unpredictable. They can be unstable-minded in their decision-making. In her world, men have always catered to their selfish needs.

"Wren, George wants a baby badly to the point it does not have to be with me. You know, we own the hair salon. Lately, I have been going through. I look at these women walk in and flirt their way to the barber side of the salon. I wonder if my husband is looking at them because he is no longer looking at me. He barely compliments me anymore."

"Wait, Cartel. You two just celebrated an anniversary. We just talked about all this stuff, and it bothers me that you didn't mention any of this to me. You made it seem like marriage was great. Furthermore, you are allowing envy to take control of your thoughts. George is not thinking about those hot-headed women parading through the barbershop. " Wren sipped her wine again.

"I guess I did not look at it as envy, but that is fair to say when I see women pregnant and carrying babies to full term. I feel less of a woman at times."

"Hey, I understand all of that, but you are never less regardless of whether you have a baby. You have accomplished much and have wonderful things in store. You are a leader."

"Thanks, and I did not mention this to you earlier because you must speak life into your marriage, Wren. I do not want to talk terrible things about my marriage; that allows the devil grounds to stir up," Cartel sipped her wine and then placed it on the table. "Enough about my marriage. Are you happy in this new marriage of yours?"

"I am fine, Cartel. I am inside it, so it is what it is now."

"Wow! It sounds like a happy union thus far. You are correct; marriage is not a relationship you get out of whenever you feel like it. It is a life-long commitment, sis."

"So, tell me about this Proverbs 31 woman. My husband seems to glow when he mentions this ideal woman."

"Listen, that Proverbs 31 woman your husband spoke about is in the Bible; of course, it is Proverbs 31. You are already a confident woman. He admires the self-love and self-respect that you have for yourself. Yet this woman is another level, sis. He hopes you build a relationship with God to become that type of woman. She is a woman of peace and humbleness. Just know, Wren; the man is the head. That means he is the protector and provider. He makes the final decisions on the family structure because he is responsible for his wife and family. As written in I Corinthians, the eleventh chapter."

Wren laughed aloud. "You make it seem difficult. We came from the hard, girl; how much more do I need? Tell me something. I am trying to figure out how the Proverbs 31 lady takes hits, punches from her husband, and remains humble and great."

"God's strength. As a Christian, I still fight hard to be that woman, okay? She is rooted in God; she wears the full armor of God. She knows when to speak and when not to speak. She admires her husband and does not talk about her husband. Another thing, when you disagree, as in healthy disagreements, you are to solve things before the sun goes down. As in, never go to bed angry. And it would be best if you got into keeping your marriage private. Wait, did you say hits and punches from her husband? I just caught that part."

"Yes, I did. I fell off somewhere Cartel. I feel like I do not know who I am anymore. My life was happy and simple. Now, I find myself trying to please this man all day, every single day. I am trying to learn how to be a woman or a wife in school. Everything I do is wrong to him. I aggravate him so much."

"Wait, are you saying Casanova is abusing you, friend? I need to make sure I hear this correctly?"

"Well, I am not sure if it is abuse because he told me that the husband is in authority. It is his way of helping me become a better woman, and I thought I was a great woman at one point in my life. I have never heard these words from any man I've dated in the past. For example, during our last night in Hawaii, we talked about what would happen next for us. While he did not take away my design career, he said that if I cannot maintain my career, raise our children and be his wife, my career must go." Wren placed her wine glass on the table. The thought of what had been happening in her life was overwhelming. She was unsure how the words sounded to Cartel or if she explained it correctly. She searched for validation and looked for Cartel to provide it.

"Okay, I can understand the part of wanting children sooner than later; you two are older. Yet, I am still stuck on the abuse part. I have been observant of Casanova's character; he treats you like a queen around me."

"I know he does. And, I might be saying all the wrong word choices. I am so confused these days. I do not know if I am coming or going. I feel like I made a mistake, but I feel drawn to this man. I have never been this connected to a man in my life. I want to make him happy, and I do not know how."

"Well, that happens when a woman has sex with a man. We get drawn into them; our souls become one. This is part of why women should wait until marriage to have sex—having sex before marriage can blind us to what a man brings to the table. It can place a Band-Aid on the red flags. I have witnessed some women choose the wrong man and lose their minds. Do I need to have a conversation with Mr. Casanova?"

"I am not sure, Cartel. It all points to this God you all serve. He is something else. It sounds as though he thinks of women as servants. If so, I cannot do it, sis. Cas expects me to cook, clean, pick out his clothes, iron, do laundry and still manage my career. His house cleaner from his Hinsdale home is helping me clean my house, but still. Pregnancy is something I cannot do. I do not want children. I never did."

"Are you kidding me? First off, God used women throughout the Bible to do important things. And not, as in slavery, but as leaders and messengers to get things done as he intended. Do not get me started. God created men as the head, but they are not superior. God does not think less of us, but we are to follow our husband's lead; that is just how it is. Also, ONLY if God is leading him. We, women, get it twisted, allowing a man who God is NOT leading to lead us. Those men can only lead us to the pit of hell. A man must not only know the word but also be a doer of the word. The classification is to be Knowledge-filled, and Spirit-filled."

"I know, but what if I don't follow his lead?" Wren questioned.

"It is not good for your marriage at all. You made a promise with Casanova before the Lord when you married him. Before marriage, these conversations should have been discussed. We, women, must stop accepting just any hand in marriage. If he is actively seeking God, he will do right by you. Casanova speaks so highly of the Lord that it is hard to view him as an abuser. Listen, do not worry about all this right now. Just enjoy your husband."

Wren halted the conversation, turning on a movie for them to watch. In the back of her mind, she worried about her marriage decision. She often thought about her brother Steven. He wanted to approve of the man Wren decided to marry. He understood that marriage was not in her plans, so he was not too involved when she met Casanova. Had he known she would marry Casanova so fast, he would have been on Casanova's heels. Wren finished her glass of wine.

Cartel, not focused on the movie, pondered Wren's words about Casanova's character. She silently prayed, hoping Casanova was not abusing her friend. She was not good with holding back words from rolling off her tongue, especially regarding women and abuse. She knew it was best to go home as soon as the movie ended to avoid conflict between her and Casanova. And Lord knows if Steven found out, he would kill Casanova with his bare hands.

Steven was like a pistol, ready to fire off at anyone who tried to hurt Wren. He had been her protector. Steven was not one to trust people easily. He was the kind of person who felt everyone came with intent. He felt their father, who turned out not to be their father, came to get their mother involved in the drug game. He hated that man. He hated any man who would allow a woman to take the blame for them, particularly a woman with children. Casanova would not be an easy win for Steven. They only met twice.

After the movie ended, Cartel decided to go home. She hugged Wren. "Everything is going to be okay; you understand me?"

"I know it will." Wren hugged her back and watched her to her car. It was not that Wren wanted to end her marriage with Casanova, but that she needed help understanding him and why he often got angry with her.

The same evening, while in bed with Casanova. Wren felt the need to revisit the talk of starting a family. She noted she was not ready to add children to her career and take care of them full-time. "Cas, are you sleeping yet?"

"Answer is no because I know you are deeply thinking about something again. Just like you were last night. I am wondering how many more nights my wife will sit up in bed as I struggle around to find comfort. Does this marriage bother you that much?"

"Indeed, it does. It has nothing to do with you, but your hopes of starting a family soon are unrealistic. I have not given kids any thought because I never wanted to marry. Well, I never wanted children either. This is a huge and fast change in my life, and frankly, it makes me angry. I have worked hard to get where I am today, and I do not want anything to interfere. Am I mean, or do I sound selfish?"

"If you need to ask, then you already know the answer. You are making sense, but yes, you sound selfish. You sound just like a single woman. I think we ought to go to bed now." Casanova was done with the conversation before it got started. Having conversations with Wren as such often lead to a physical encounter. He struggled to understand how easy it became for him to strike her. The abuse was not his norm.

"Fine, as long as you understand, I do not want any children for us anytime soon."

"That's what you're asking me or telling me?" Casanova inquired, rising from the bed to look at her. Wren immediately felt threatened by his tone and movement.

She said, "I am responsible for this body, not you. So, that means I tell you, Casanova."

Casanova whipped a slap across her face. She grabbed her face and clenched her fist, now angry. With evil intent, she stared at him, ready to defend herself.

"Wren, this is not going very well," Casanova placed his head in his hands. His intention was not to swing at Wren, but he struggled with her authoritative tone. His mother never raised her voice or told his father what she would or would not do. "You have no idea how to be a married woman, and I knew better. Wren, you cannot speak to me like you are the head. I should not have swung at you. I am sorry. I realize now that I made a mistake by rushing into marriage."

She relaxed her fist. "Cas, let's just annul this before someone gets hurt."

"Listen, I cannot take back my vows from God and say it was a mistake. Our yay is our yay, and our nay is our nay. We are stuck in this thing. You can express your views and concerns as much as you like. I shall always listen and respect you, but you will never make the ultimate decision for us."

Wren, still holding her face, responded. "I am not deciding for us, Casanova. I am deciding for myself. If you got away and divorced me tomorrow, I would be stuck with that kid. Unlike most women, I do not hang on to a man's every word. Men change their minds whenever they feel like it. My so-called father exposed me to those actions as a child. Having kids is an enormous undertaking. I must be ready for that long-term commitment. You cannot force that on me because I agreed to your hand in marriage. And why do you always have to swing and hit me when I upset you? Is this what your God allows you to do or instructs you to do?"

Casanova sighed, "No, he does not allow me to hit you. I am not sure where the physical factor is stemming from, Wren. I tend to lose it when you speak to me so authoritatively. I feel this will get ugly, and I do not want it to go there. Let us sleep on it and discuss it tomorrow, please."

"Right, again, as long as you know, I will not be having our children anytime soon!" Wren picked up a pocket mirror from her nightstand. She looked at her face hoping it was not forming a bruise. She glanced at Casanova, who had already turned away from her to lie back down. *I cannot get accustomed to abuse,* she thought. *I will kill this man first before I continue to allow his hands to beat my face.*

Casanova, who could not sleep, was perplexed by her. He knew marrying her would be a tough fight but never imagined having to place his hands on her for control. He never witnessed his father having to beat his mother. His mother was obedient to his father's demands and served accordingly. Wren was undoubtedly a piece of work. Casanova knew he had to get her in line before his mother, Anna, found this out. If Anna heard her speak to him in that tone, she would argue her down. A woman is not authoritative over a man. He shook his head and whispered, *"God help me, and please, please, please forgive me."* reaching for the lamp to turn off the light.

Wren was still not at rest. Her mind raced to find a way to cancel this marriage contract. She did not wish to break Casanova's heart, but she did not want to hurt her own either by doing things she was not ready to do. Now it was she that squirmed in the bed for comfort.

She wondered if her life experiences impacted her ways of thinking. If her dad had not left her, would she feel this way about Casanova? She was unsure if Casanova had it in him to leave his child or children in his heart.

People never really know their spouse or what they can do. People do not know themselves or how they would react to a situation until they have experienced it.

Broken7

The following Saturday, the hair salon was packed with at least thirty women by 8 am. Cartel took two bites of her bagel with cream cheese before tossing it in the garbage.

Most women were part of a wedding party for her client, Tracy, whose wedding was at 3 pm. All hands were on deck; the hairstylist team rotated the group of women from the washbowl to the hand dryer to Cartel's chair.

The hair salon, decorated in pink and lavender décor, was bustling, surrounded by blossoms of cyclamen winter flowers. A medium-built Caucasian woman with short blonde hair, Susan Welling's owned a flower shop just a block from Cartel's salon. Susan was a weekly client of Cartel's who loved to fill the hair salon with fresh flowers and plants. Cartel often would argue with Susan as she knew the bulk of the deliveries took away from Susan's revenue. They agreed that Cartel would give Susan thirty percent discounts on her hair care in exchange for fresh flowers and sometimes replacement of dead plants. Susan entered the salon with a fresh new bouquet arrangement. "These are for the bride-to-be and her crew," Susan said, bringing in a few boxes.

"How pretty are those, "Cartel beamed. "See, I needed you around, Ms. Susan, when I married several years ago. You truly have a gift in arrangements."

"Ms. Susan, I agree with Cartel. You made my day so much better coming through with these arrangements. These are gorgeous! And it coordinates so well with our dresses. Thank you so much for the gift." Tracy admired it with gratitude.

"My pleasure Tracy. I wish I had a chance to do this for my daughter." Susan responded, rubbing her hand across a small dash on her forehead.

"You have a daughter, Ms. Susan?" Tracy asked.

"I sure do. My daughter is about your age." Susan confirmed.

"Why haven't we met this daughter, Ms. Susan?" Cartel asked, adding the final changes to Tracy's hair.

"That girl is like her mother; she is doing well. She is busy, but we talk often."

"Well, that is good. One day, you should bring her by to meet everyone. It is a shame, you have been my client for almost two years, and I think you have spoken about her once or twice."

"No, I have mentioned her more than that now. I am immensely proud of her success. I admire her dearly."

"You might be right. I heard you say that before." Cartel added. "Okay, Tracy, you look fine like wine, my friend. I wish you nothing but blessings and happiness in your marriage. You need to get going now. Your style is free today, my love. My gift to you. Now, get married!"

"You are the best; I love my hair!" Tracy exclaimed. "Will you please have my bridesmaid out on time?"

"We are going to keep on moving them out. You go on now. Get to the church before your mother calls my shop looking for you."

"Because you know she will too. My mother has been calling me since last night, telling me to be on time." Tracy retorted.

As Tracy exited the shop, a heavy-set Latino woman entered. Her long jet-black curly hair slicked back into a ponytail. Wearing dark sunglasses and a baseball cap, the woman sat in one of the waiting area chairs, muttering words.

"Garcia, what is wrong with you, my love?" Cartel asked, walking up to her.

"I am done with men. All he does is cheat on me. When I confront him, he lies and always wants to fight me. Whelp, today was the last time, Cartel. My girl, Yesenia, told me to leave that man, well, all men alone anyway. She would take care of me, and I trust her."

"Whoa, wait a second. I get it about Jose. He needs to keep his hands off you. You must do what is best for you and little Maggie. Regarding Yesenia, are you saying you want to be a lesbian now?"

"Yesenia and I have been spending a lot of time together, Cartel. And I know you will condemn me with the Church of God stuff, but I feel so safe with Yesenia."

"Could it be that you feel safe with Yesenia because she has been your best friend since you two were five years old?"

"Partly, but Yesenia is correct to say men do not love us, women. They use us for sex and to cook and clean up behind them. Give them babies, and cheat on us."

"Are you here for an appointment today, or are you just needing an ear to listen?"

"Both, I just made the appointment as I walked here. I had to get away from Jose. I asked Yesenia to pick me up once I got my hair done. I am not going back home. I just need to find a way to get Maggie from him."

"Well, I am glad you will be at the shop with me for a while. I must get this wedding party out before you, but I want to talk and pray with you. Are you willing to hang out longer than the norm today?"

"I will. You have always been a good person to hear me out. I appreciate you, Cartel. I will be sitting here upfront until you call me back."

"I appreciate you too, my love. And not just as my long-term client, but as a friend. A friend that I want to see do very well in life. You are like a little sister to me. I want the best for you. We will talk in a moment." Cartel told her as she walked away to finish the wedding party.

Cartel began to pray. *Lord, I am going to need your help with this one. I need the right words to say to my friend Yasmin Garcia. She is wounded and has been for years; only you can give her the love and guidance she needs to live through this. Please use me as a vessel to help my friend.*

As you know, the plans you have for her, as Jeremiah 29:11 reminds us. Just as the verse speaks to the descendants of Israel, who were set free, and the promise you made to Abraham to bless his people. I know this holds for us today. You can free her from this situation, salvation through Christ Jesus. And Lord,

Broken7

show her the plans you have for her life. Please help me, to help her find you in Jesus' name. Amen.

After Cartel closed the shop, she met up with Wren for dinner. Cartel had texted Wren earlier, inviting her to the after-work spot to meet and talk. The abuse Wren mentioned still bothered Cartel from a week ago.

Wren noticed that Cartel was quieter than usual as they sat at their table. She looked worried or troubled. "Are you feeling okay, girl?"

"I feel fine, but I have so much on mind right now."

"Like what? Can I help you with something?" Wren asked, placing a cloth napkin across her lap.

"You know me. I am not particularly eager to discuss people's business. I try to take it to my grave when they confide in me unless they tell me differently. I have you and another person heavy in my prayers right now."

"Well, consider me as you, and open, sis! Besides, who am I going to tell anyway?"

"It is not about that, Wren; it relates more to not gossiping, per the Bible. We must be careful with

Broken7

words. There is the scripture in Proverbs 11:13. A talebearer revealeth secrets, but he that is of a faithful spirit concealeth the matter."

"Okay, do not tell me who, but tell me what the problem is. Will that help?"

"Yes, it would. I guess that would be okay. A client is considering becoming a lesbian. I am concerned not only from a biblical stance but also that she makes this decision out of fear."

"Girl, Garcia has always been into Yesenia. And Yesenia has always been into Garcia. Stop the nonsense that has nothing to do with Jose beating on her. I thought you had a real issue."

"How did you know I was speaking about Garcia?"

"You think I have been gone from home too long, huh? Although I just moved back home, I still know Garcia well. She and that best friend have always liked one another."

"Wren, she will displease God if she goes that route. I do not want to see my friends or family displeasing God. Plus, she is doing this out of fear. She no longer wants to date men out of fear. All men do not abuse women. She has that conclusion."

"Here you go with that stuff. I am the wrong person to speak to about action figure types of Gods and stuff. I cannot help with that part. I am telling you not to worry about your girl Garcia; they have considered that for many moons."

"I knew I should have kept my mouth shut because I can no longer listen to this nonsense about God. Let us, please, change the subject. We need to point this back at you, Wren." Cartel said, refocusing on Wren's issue.

"Whelp, according to you, my issue relates to your God too, so throw it on me already."

The server walks up to greet them. "Hello ladies, may I start you off with something to drink or appetizers?"

"Yes, please, spinach dip and bread. I will also take strawberry lemonade for my drink," Wren began.

"I will share her appetizer, but I will take a Pepsi for my drink." Cartel finished. Cartel hesitated a moment before starting her conversation again with Wren. Her constant jokes about God were beginning to wear very thin.

"Are you going to give me a bible lesson or not? You, staring at me, is quite spooky." Wren added.

"I am not even hungry anymore, Wren. And, I do not have a bible story or scripture in me to give you now. You make light of everything. My pregnancy! You gave me no positive feedback except when you said George would not leave me for my pregnancy issues. You are making light of your marriage. Now, you are making light of Garcia's situation. Garcia is only about twenty-eight years old. She got raised in foster care just like you and me. We took her under our wing because she is like a little sister. What has gotten into you, friend? You are so different now?"

"First of all, you came in here talking about Garcia as if she was just your client. She is like a little sister to us. I knew what was going on with her because she told me. She called my phone and left me a voicemail about helping her with an escape plan. She wants to grab Maggie from Jose and hide out at my house. Your problem is carrying everyone's issues on your shoulder. Having stress is why you cannot stay pregnant. I did not make light of your pregnancy issue. I heard you out, my friend!"

The server slid their appetizers and drinks onto the table. Their body language displayed aggravation. With that, he decided to say less and quickly walked away.

"Ok. Calm down. I might have spoken out of frustration. My load is heavy." Cartel acknowledged, taking a sip of her pop.

"No, let me finish. I stay quiet when I do not have the right words to say. I try not to speak out of term. And last, my problems are causing a shift in my life, an uncomfortable one at that. I am shielding a marriage from my brother Steven. I have limited communication with him because I no longer know who I am. I do not know what a regular life feels like anymore because all I do daily is fight with a man who tells me he loves me and slaps me around."

"One minute you say he is abusing you, the next minute you say I am simply confused. Well, let me help you with that. That is abuse if he places his hands on you during intense arguments. And I want you to understand that is not okay and not biblical. No one can help you in that situation but you. I say that because if I tell the police about him, you say it is not happening, and you are confused, then no one can save you."

Wren silenced in deep thought. Going to the police about a Black man is like pulling the trigger on a gun. The outcome for Casanova would be a ruined acting career or a body bag. Casanova was very apologetic each time he snapped and swung. Wren was not into ending someone's life or career. Especially one who was only trying to love her.

The ladies sat silently, eating spinach dip and bread while exchanging very few words. Both women were not operating out of their usual element. They understood they had reached a foreign territory and were experiencing something new simultaneously, making it harder to support each other.

After dinner, they agreed to call it a night. Wren gathered her things from the table as Cartel's cell phone rang. Ignoring the call from Yesenia, Garcia's friend was best now. She had no energy to advise anyone.

Cartel and Wren walked to their cars still with minimal words to say.

"Please know, everything will work out regarding the baby, Cartel." Wren encouraged.

"Yes, I know. And please know that I love you and have your back regarding Casanova. We will get you out of this situation."

"Girl, Casanova cannot beat me up for real. He is such a light swinger, laughable, but I still do not like being slapped. I fear knocking him out if he does not stop it." Wren laughed aloud. She wanted to kill the thought of being abused. She did not wish to have Cartel worried about it any longer.

"I won't even attempt to laugh at that," Cartel responded. "You all should not be swinging at each other. But at least it gives me peace knowing you still feel safe. That was confirmation he is not beating you, correct?"

"Casanova has slapped me about five times in the last six months. Once we wrestled to the floor, I pinned him up, and it was over. He apologized before we went to bed each time. I do not know what I am experiencing with him. I am trying not to run from this mess. I used to be so happy with him, Cartel. His mother's influence is the root of our fights. Anyway, I am trying to stay committed and learn to fight."

"Well, I would never advise staying in an unsafe, unhealthy environment either. I have known you for many years, Wren. I could read you so well before. The words you say now this is not your norm. You used to speak confidently, and now you backtrack on every word."

"I know that I do, and I cannot understand why. You say I speak confidently, but Cas said I speak unlearned."

"He said that?" Cartel asked. "See, I want to go hard and involve Steven. I want to go hard and address Casanova myself, but you double back and say things jokingly like you are making things up. Telling me that he slapped you five times but then calling him a punk with a lightweight swinger makes me think you two have disagreements but nothing more."

"Well, he has slapped me around a few times. I just admitted that. And I've also pinned him up because he cannot fight for real." Wren smiled.

"George and I play fight all the time. Not during an agreement, though. I throw pillows at him, cups, or whatever is in sight when he gets on my nerves, but not during a disagreement. We are in a good space when we are wrestling around." Cartel's cell phone rings again.

"Girl, someone needs to talk to you. Answer that phone!" Wren demanded, opening her car door.

Cartel answered to the voice of Yesenia. Yesenia cried and yelled through the phone as she explained Garcia's attempt to rescue her daughter Maggie from Jose ended badly. Wren was listening closely alongside. "Which hospital? I am on my way!" Cartel assured, hanging up the phone. She jumped in her car and headed to the hospital emergency room.

Wren heard just enough to follow behind Cartel. Wren always tended to make light of situations to cover pain, but there was no time for light jokes in this case. Yasmin Garcia was a little sister to both women. Wren wished more than anything for Yasmin to come through simply fine.

Two weeks later:

Garcia got released from the hospital. She suffered a fractured rib cage and other bruises. The hospitalist was concerned about her developing pneumonia, which is reasonable for fractured rib cages. After carefully monitoring that and Garcia's other health conditions, the team decided to send her home. They advised her to follow up with the orthopedic physician on call in a few days. Since Garcia was unemployed and without medical insurance, Cartel called up a favor from her first cousin and physician, Dr. Liza Littlejohn. She asked her to help manage Garcia's care. And, of course, she agreed. Cartel and Garcia entered the exam room.

"Thank you, Dr. Littlejohn, for seeing me today without health insurance." Garcia said, taking a seat on the exam table."

"I am not worried about that, Yasmin. I mean, Garcia, your preferred name. My goal is to get you back in shape. The orthopedic doctor on call is obligated to see you at least once. He must make sure all is healing properly. He might schedule other visits as he sees fit. Normally these things heal over time." she explained to Garcia and Cartel.

"That's great news!" Cartel responded with a smile, sitting in one of the guest chairs.

"Yes, I would agree. Also, I am writing you some prescriptions because you have diabetes; as they explained at the hospital, your numbers are concerning."

"Yes, I knew I was diabetic. I do not have insurance to afford medications."

"Garcia, there are programs to help with that. I am sure my cousin, Cartel, knows many of them."

"I do know of a few programs, Garcia. I wish you had told me this beforehand. Diabetes is nothing to play around with, girl. Go ahead and wait for me in the waiting room. I am going to wrap up with my cousin. I will bring out your patient summary and prescriptions."

"Thank you again!" Garcia said, walking out of the room.

"So, should I have her schedule a follow-up with you too? I know how you act about uninsured folks." Cartel asked.

"Yes, I genuinely want to help her. She can follow up with me in three months but needs to follow up with the ortho sooner." Liza responded.

"Wow, which is shocking coming from you. To genuinely want to help someone of color."

"I know where you are going with this Cartel. I am not a bad person. I am not particularly eager to waste my time either. Typically, it is the Black people who waste my time, Cartel. Garcia is Latino. We have had these conversations a million times."

"Which is why I am asking you questions. I know Garcia is not black, but she is Latino. And let us not forget I am still half-Black, so watch what you say about my people. My father was as Black as they come."

"Cartel? Really! Please do not bring this into my private practice. I am not racially prejudiced, so stop standing hard for your people. Statistics show Black people have the highest percentages in several diseases. It is not because of their skin. It is because most do not care about themselves. I have Black patients; some are in excellent health because they care. While others cancel appointments and see me once every three years; after something bad has happened. I am stating facts."

"Who's facts? Most of the statistics are falsified hype. Anyway, I am speaking to you from experience. I was in the mall with you when the Black woman fell beside us with chest pain. You, as a physician, did not help her. Instead, you argued with me, stating she does not care enough about her life. You claimed if she had routine visits, she would have known about any issue before it got to that level."

"That was three years ago. And the woman lived! Why do you continue to hold that over my head? The paramedics got there in time, and you witnessed that part. Stop reminding me of that story, please! This conversation is over. I genuinely want to help your broke friend. Is that better?"

"I am going to continue to pray for you, seriously!"

"And speaking of that prayer, add to it about this intelligent man I met on a dating application. I am going on a date with him tomorrow night. After spending three months conversating by phone, he sounds like a keeper."

"Have you seen him on video or anything?" Cartel asked, concerned.

"No, and the crazy part is he did not have a profile picture either. He said he is not into taking photos. I am not sure why I took a chance on this guy, but so far, so good."

"Okay, Dr. Liza Littlejohn. You know better than that! I will add you to my prayers. What is his name anyway?"

"His name is Henry Stallings. Sounds like a professional athlete, huh?"

"No, he sounds like a mystery. Talk to you later, cousin. I appreciate you!" Cartel responded, exiting the exam room.

When Cartel got home, she walked into her bedroom filled with flowers, balloons, cake, wine, and a hand-written card. It was not her birthday, so it took her by surprise. Her husband, George, stood awaiting her presence. She could not tell by his facial expression what led to this celebration. George took a seat on one end of the bed with a half-grin. "What is this all about?" she asked him.

"It is about you. I have been thinking, and I feel convicted. I have not been the best husband to you lately. I get so excited about becoming a father and then let down quickly. It is hard for me as a man to stay strong when I want a child so badly. If I made you feel worthless, I apologize."

"Thank you. You have not made me feel bad, but I sure am beating myself up. Do you know how often I ask God what is wrong with me? Why can't I stay pregnant? Why am I half a woman or not a woman at all? As confident as I am, I now envy other women, especially women with children. I must repent and ask God to help me with these ill feelings about myself and others. Being a Christian is a daily fight with flesh."

"Yes, that is true. We love God enough to fight our flesh daily for change. No one is perfect bae. You are doing your best as a wife, evangelist, and friend to many. I am grateful to God for having you as my life partner."

"Even if I cannot birth children for us?"

"We will figure something out. Right now, let us keep our prayers lifted and faith strong. God has the final say, and we still have time."

"Thank you, George. The flowers and everything are beautiful but thank you for being a great support. I am grateful to you as well. My man! My head!" Cartel embraced him with a hug.

"It is all good. I ran you some bathwater. Candlelight and pink and white roses surround the tub. Go in there and soak, and I will be in there to see about you soon."

"Sounds like a plan." Cartel agreed.

Chapter Three: Secret Revealed

It was about five-thirty on a winter Sunday evening. Casanova and Wren were ready to share with the family their marriage news. The guest list was short, as they invited those closest to them. Wren's guests included her brother, Steven, and his long-term girlfriend, Shai Luster. Her former college friend, Jamie Brownstone-Lee, and her husband, Karl Lee. And, of course, Cartel and her husband, George. However, Casanova's list included his parents, Anna and George. And his best friend, the unmarried and uncommitted Ryan Jake, known as naughty by nature. Lately, Ryan has kept a woman named Ginny Jonez at his side, but a commitment is yet to be determined, judging by his history.

Casanova had given his father the news while in Hawaii but had asked that he not share with his mother, Anna, until dinner. His father welcomed the marriage as he knew his son had found a great person. He needed his father's authoritativeness present as his mother received the news. However, Steven, Wren's brother, did not get informed. Casanova was optimistic about being accepted by him.

Their family and friends sat around the table eating and having sidebar conversations. Casanova signaled to one of the servers, James, to bring out the wedding bands. The couple decided not to wear their rings to the dinner table. It was part of their plan to shine attention to the announcement made by the server. Casanova looked over at his mother, Anna. She appeared to be in a good mood thus far. *Please, Lord, let her stay in a great mood.*

Wren sat nervously, patiently awaiting the server's queue. Steven was her primary concern. She hoped the news would not damage their relationship. Wren made eye contact with Cartel. Cartel could sense her nervousness. She smiled at Wren and whispered, *"I got you!"* hoping that would ease her concern. Wren smiled back at her.

"May I have your attention?" James, the server, began. The guest looked his way as he stood next to a seated Casanova. In his hands was a white satin pillow with two glistering wedding bands. "I would like to introduce Mr. and Mrs. Casanova Bryant." James lowered the pad to allow Casanova a chance to remove Wren's wedding band. He then made his way over to Wren to enable her to do the same for Casanova's wedding band.

Anna's facial expression reached a confused state. "What is this?" she asked.

Casanova rosed from his chair. On one knee, he knelt beside Wren. "Wren, for the past three weeks, well, almost four weeks, you have made me the happiest man to have you as my wife. Thank you for marrying me in the beautiful state of Hawaii. It was by far the best decision I have made in my life. From this day on, our marriage is not a secret. We are blessed to have our family and friends here tonight to welcome and bless our union. I offer a commitment to love, respect, and protect you." He placed the ring on her finger.

Wren smiled. "Thank you, Cas. I promise to stay by your side through the thick and thin with this ring. This ring bonds us for life. I appreciate you, respect you, and am grateful for you. Thank you for choosing me to be your partner for life." She placed a ring on his finger.

Everyone at the table appeared surprised. Most clapped for the couple, including Steven, while Anna did not move a muscle. Casanova took a seat back at the head of the table. "Now, who is ready for the wedding cake?" Casanova asked as the servers brought out a beautiful 3-layered white cake with pink and peach color rose illustrations. The cake; uniquely designed with Wren's favorite colors.

"Um, where is the objection part? I mean, what is going on for real." Anna asked again.

"Anna, our son got married last month while filming in Hawaii. He did ask for our blessing, and I gave it to him for both of us. " Casanova's father, Gregory, advised.

Anna, now upset, fought back her emotions. Last month, she found it strange when Casanova moved out of the home he built to move in with Wren. Yet, she never thought he would marry without her blessing, let alone her presence. Feeling heartbroken, she glanced at

Casanova, smiling and chatting with others. *How could he ignore my questions and concerns?*

"How are you feeling, Anna?" Gregory asked. He noticed the sadness on his wife's face.

"Gregory, I cannot sit here and enjoy this foolishness. I want to go home." Anna expelled, facing him.

"We are not going home until this evening concludes. It is our son's private dinner gathering to celebrate their union. You should be congratulating your new daughter-in-law and embracing her in hugs. She is a beautiful woman."

Steven rose from the table. "Um, Wren, can I speak to you for a moment in the kitchen?"

"Yes, sure, bro." Wren followed him to the kitchen. She was genuinely concerned about his feelings now that the news was out.

"So, this is what we do?" he questioned, leaning against the kitchen island.

"Bro, it just happened. I had no plans to marry Casanova without your blessings. We were in Hawaii, it was a beautiful evening, and it just happened. There was no prior engagement announcement you missed; it just happened."

"I get it. It just happened, but some things should not just happen. You do not even know this man. How is he treating you? Has he changed since you have been his wife almost a month?"

"No, bro. He is a fantastic guy. He has taught me the bible and helped me to understand the wife's role. All is well."

"All is well, huh? Teaching you the bible? Since when did you start believing in Christ? You lost that belief when we were children. You did not want me to touch a bible back in the day after dad left us."

"You still call him dad? He is not our father, remember? The DNA test provided the evidence he needed to leave us."

"Yeah, but he and mom are back together now. Both have apologized a million times for leaving us, so I am over it. Now, back to you. I cannot give you my blessing, sis! I do not know the dude that well. I got my eyes on him too. I do not care about wedding paper. *I care about my* sister."

"I hear you, bro, loud and clear," Casanova responded, walking into the kitchen. He was anxious to hear Steven's thoughts about him. "I just came in to chat with you. I know that things happened quickly, but I got your sister. She is safe."

"Yeah, ok, but you heard what I said. I do not support this union yet. A man who would drift a woman away from her family and marry her without family support appears fishy. Real men do not make moves like that. If you are hiding something or if you change upon my sister in any type of way. I am at you, bro. That is not a threat either."

"Understood. No violence, man, we are good." Casanova reached his hand out to shake Steven's hand.

"Yep, you two be happy now." Steven shook his hand and exited the kitchen.

Wren, a bit relieved, quickly fell into Casanova's arms. "You good, love?" he asked.

"Not really, I feel like I lied to my brother about some things, but I will be alright."

"Hey, do not ever lie to anyone to defend our love. Ok?"

"Yes, but it was a little deeper than that, but it is all good again. How is your mother holding up?"

"I have been avoiding her. I will not make eye contact with her. I am trying to enjoy this evening. My boy, Ryan, cuss me out because I could have told him sooner than today, but he is happy for me. He said he was thinking about marrying Ginny too. I laughed because he was lying through his teeth. He only said that because she was sitting next to him."

"Yeah, Jamie and Karl gave us their full support. And of course, Cartel's husband George already knew from Cartel. They were just here for added support. However, I am shocked that Garcia did not show up."

"I am sure she is fine. I am going to head back in there with our guest. How about you?" he released her from his arms.

"I need a moment. I will be back in there shortly."

"Ok, if you need me. I am not too busy and never too far."

Wren laughed. "Noted!" she responded as he walked away. *He is not too busy and never too far.* Wren battled not sharing the abuse issue she encountered from Casanova. She pondered seeing a psychologist who could help her validate her thoughts and emotions. Cartel was correct to say there was confusion with the term abuse. One minute he was abusive; the next, he was Mr. Everything. There was no doubt; Wren felt confused. She wanted to trust her decision and that Casanova was a great man. Then there was this inside feeling that told her differently.

"Why are you still in this kitchen while everyone is now dancing to music and enjoying themselves?" Jamie asked as she and Cartel entered the kitchen.

"Well, everyone except Ms. Anna. She is at that table staring at everyone until this moment." Cartel added.

"What moment?" Wren asked.

"Mr. Gregory just pulled her into a conversation with Casanova. Hopefully, after their conversation, she will be in better spirits. We just came to check on you. Steven is still with the fellas, so we assumed all went well with that conversation, correct?"

"Yeah, of course, but Steven threatened him before he agreed to allow us to be happy. I must give him credit for that well-behaved action because I expected worse."

"Well, that's great news, right?" Cartel exclaimed with a huge smile. "We had George on standby as a bodyguard prepared to break up a fight."

"Well, I am glad that was not needed." Jamie agreed. "So, how do you feel, my friend? I am here to check on your spirit."

"I do not know, Jamie. I love this guy, but he pushes children on me fast."

"I get it, though. You and Casanova married at an older age, so he wants them, babies, on the way. It took Karl and me years to get pregnant. I remember being so jealous of my younger sister, Kimmel. Remember when she had a child before me?"

"Wait, girl. Are you telling us you are pregnant?" Cartel asked, catching the hint.

"Yes, we found out last week. I knew I was pregnant but did not want to be disappointed. So, I waited a long time to schedule a doctor's appointment. We are twelve weeks pregnant."

"That is so exciting. I know you and I have battled with this for years, but it gives me much faith to hear this great news!" Cartel hugged her.

"Thank you, yes, Karl and I have been married almost eight years. God is faithful."

"Yes, he is." Cartel agreed, stepping back to look at her.

"I am happy for you too because you both wanted children; however, I am not sure if I do," Wren added.

"Oh, then yes, Wren, a conversation with your husband is necessary. It must be a joint agreement because children will change your world. You must be ready for them."

"How old is your nephew now? About six, right?" Cartel asked.

"Yes, Jordan is the center of my joy. I got over Kimmel's jealousy when I looked at my nephew. My husband is so attached to him. We feel like he is our son. Kimmel is back in school again, this time to be a lawyer."

"Girl, you have a full house already. Does Kimmel still live with you? I know the twins are there; Amiya and Riya; they are teenagers, right?" Cartel continued to ask questions, curious about Jamie's sanity.

"If you are trying to ask if my mother is still on drugs. Yes, Cartel. My mother is a full-blown heroin addict. We sporadically see her. Karl and I still take care of my sixteen-year-old twin sisters. And yes, my twenty-five-year-old sister, Kimmel, still lives with us.

"No, I was more concerned about your sanity. Being married for eight years and raising your siblings for eight is an enormous undertaking. You two did not have a chance to be newlyweds. Karl married you and committed to raising your siblings with you. You have a good man by your side. I am so glad you can now give him a child of his own."

"Hey, she's making that registered nurse money, and her man is a physician assistant, so they can manage it financially," Wren added.

"Girl, please, not with my bougie twin sisters. I must work about twenty overtime hours weekly to keep up with them." Jamie laughed but was serious. "Back to you, Wren. Besides the request to have children quickly, are you good with everything else? You seemed quiet at the table. You and I have not spoken in almost five months. I knew you had a man, and life changed, so I was not concerned. However, I did discern something at the table."

"No, I am good. I was just nervous about my brother. Let's make our way back out, dance, and enjoy ourselves. Tonight is my marriage celebration. Let us have fun!' Wren responded, leading the ladies back out into the dining room.

The following day, Cartel was busy at the salon prepping to open for the day. Susan walked in with a fresh floral arrangement for the front windowpane.

"That is beautiful, Susan. I love it! It matches the colors. It is hard to keep up with Chicago's seasons. We get about four weeks of summer, two weeks of fall, forty-eight weeks of winter, and two weeks of spring."

"Sounds about right. We get cooler days than warm, that is for sure. Are you ready for me at the washbowl, or do you want me to sit? I am a bit early." Susan asked as she placed the flowers on the windowpane.

"Give me about ten minutes. I keep calling my friend Garcia on her phone, but she is not answering. I need to make sure she is all right."

"Oh yes, I heard about that. You know, people are always gossiping around the town. Did they release her from the hospital?"

"Yes, and she followed up with her doctor, but she did not show up at our friend Wren's marriage celebration, which was rare. I am concerned."

"Wow! Well, I hope everything is ok. And, congrats to Wren. She is a beautiful lady, and I wish her nothing but happiness. I have seen her wearing some beautiful gown pieces on the internet and traveling with her beau, Casanova. They make a beautiful couple."

"Yes, they do. I am happy for Wren and Casanova. Garcia did not answer again," Cartel told her, putting down her cell phone. "It is early in the morning; I will try her again later. You can come over to the washbowl."

"Do not worry, Cartel. I am hopeful Garcia is fine." Susan encouraged sitting at the washbowl chair.

"Thanks. So, did you hear about the mom and daughter with that one celebrity chick held at the Hyatt last weekend? I thought about your daughter and you. I wondered if you had seen or heard the advertisement and got a chance to go."

"Yes, I heard it on the radio. I heard it late, though. I would need to give my daughter a two or three-week heads up; her calendar stays full."

"Understood. That hotel makes those dinners with different celebrity moms and daughters every month. You should check their calendar to see when the next one is scheduled."

"That is a great idea, thank you," Susan agreed, "By the way, I have a question. I was speaking to this woman who got adopted at an early age. She mentioned having trouble obtaining her original birth certificate. I know that you collaborate with many broken women. Have you ever encountered this with any women you have witnessed?"

"No, ma'am. Not with the women I support." Cartel responded, positioning Susan's head in the bowl.

"Well, a word from the wise. Your mother would be immensely proud to have a daughter like you. This community admires you."

"Thanks, Ms. Susan, which is something I have wanted to hear for many years. Sometimes it gets difficult being in this world alone without my parents. My father's family is everything, although none took me in after grandma died. I still attend all the family gatherings and cookouts. I have gathered all the soul food recipes from my grandma and aunts, but I struggle with feeling connected to them."

Broken7

"Yeah, that sounds tough," Susan responded as Cartel washed her hair.

Then, there is my mother's side of the family. They do not treat me like family for some reason. I feel like I have nothing in common with those people. Anyway, God is faithful. He blessed me with a great husband, and my best friend, Wren. Wren and I have been through hell and hot water together, but we will be forever friends, forever sisters."

"And that is beautiful. Although I wish your story, at least with your mom's side, was not so weird. You have got this, though. You have made it thus far!"

"With God, nothing is impossible." Cartel reminded, pulling Susan's head up to towel dry.

Cartel often thought of her mother and how her life would have been with her around. Another reason she fought so hard with Wren about not including her mother, Sharon, in her life. However, Wren ignored her as usual. Wren does not understand how fortunate she is to have a chance to know her mother.

Cartel moved Susan to her chair to blow dry her hair. Garcia walked into the salon with the broadest grin. Cartel looked at her for a moment; she examined for new bruises or evidence of trauma. "Where have you been?" she then asked.

"I have been fatigued, but I did not forget you offered me a job to wash hair. So, here I am, ready for the day."

"And you're late, like an hour late. Anyway, you had us worried about you. How come you did not attend Wren's dinner last night?"

"I was sleeping. I had asked Yesenia to wake me up, but she did not. She said I must have needed the rest since I did not wake up alone."

"Well. I will not argue that point. Your body does need rest to recuperate. Suppose you could start folding the towels that I pulled from the dryer. I scattered my appointments today to allow time to train you and be respectful of my client's time. So, let us start with the towels."

"Cool!" Garcia made her way to the backroom to fold towels.

Meanwhile, Wren was busy designing new after five gowns for a satin piece collection at home in her lab. The sounds of smooth jazz played from her IPAD surround sound device. She developed her best dresses, relaxed, and listening to jazz. Last night, after the celebration dinner, she and Casanova enjoyed their alone time. It was the first time that she could sleep without any concerns in a long time.

"Morning baby, I see you are up and at it early!" Casanova joined her in the lab.

"Yes, last night was a great night. I am glad our family and close friends are now aware, and life feels somewhat normal again."

"It does. Also, I am glad that you and I are on one accord about having our first baby sooner than later. We fought about that thing for a minute."

"Casanova, please. I want to enjoy the moment of peace. I did not decide on this baby; you did. If it happens, then it does."

"What a way to speak life into existence. You are so unlearned. So, you say you do not care about me enough to bring my seed?"

"Here we go!" Wren sat down her pencils. She turned around on the stool to face her husband. "All I said is, if it happens, it does."

"You are supposed to want it to happen. A good wife is supportive of her husband's decisions for the family. Must you doubt my character? Do you think I am not wise enough to make family decisions? Why would you be so against it if not?"

"I do not doubt you, but I am starting to think you doubt yourself. I am dealing with the unknown fear of the future. You and I have more troubled times than good. If you change your mind about us one day, I will get left with a child."

"I would never leave my child in your custody. Are you serious? Do you think I would do that? I am smarter than that, love. If your brain were in a bird, it would fly backward. You are a confused woman. I would not subject my child to that misery."

"Wow, you say that often. I would believe you if I did not have a college education and made intelligent business decisions. At least I can make decisions without consulting my mother."

Casanova, now offended, stared at Wren. He thought of many things he could say to destroy Wren's confidence but halted. "Is that how you feel, Wren? Am I mama's boy? Well, at least I have memories with my mother. As for you, your mother's memories are of her in a prison cell. No wonder you are misguided. Your mother was misguided to allow a man to bring her down like that."

Wren jumped up from the stool. She got in his face and yelled, "I am leaving you. Get out of my house today!" She grabbed her phone and clicked on her brother Steve's number.

"Wren, do you think I will lose sleep if you leave me? You are not suitable for anything but sex! You are not as intelligent as I previously thought. Your dream is as tiny as a celebrity clothes designer. Who does that, anyway? Stupid, bi**h!"

"Oh, now you want to take it to the streets. Calling me cuss words like the brothas on the street would do. What happened to your Christian walk now? I knew your God was fake. All you so-called Christians who claim to be holier than thou are wolves in sheep's clothing. As soon as someone tests your spirit, bruise your ego, the real you come forth."

Casanova punched Wren to the floor. Her phone flew across the room. He instantly lost self-control. As Wren struggled to get back up, he kicked her back down, shoving his foot in her face. Her nose bled. Casanova, now startled, knelt beside her. He used his shirt to help with the nosebleed. "Baby, I am so sorry! I did not mean to say those harsh words. I am not sure how I lost control."

Wren pushed away from him. With tears flowing, she cradled herself using his shirt to clear her nose bleed. So sternly, she fought hard not to search for her phone and call her brother Steven. The ending result would be deadly if she did. Steven would brutally murder the man and be in prison for life. Instead, she sat cross-legged, holding her face between her legs, pondering her thoughts.

In disbelief of his actions, Casanova watched Wren for about 10-12 minutes before leaving the lab. He was hurt. He was offended by Wren's words. He felt broken that he was now a woman beater. He had never hit a woman previously and never struggled with control. Then again, other women did not have a voice like Wren either. He wanted to understand why he needed to smack his wife whenever she raised her voice. *What is wrong with me?* He questioned himself, walking through the house.

The doorbell rang as Casanova entered the middle floor of their home. It was Steven and Shai; Casanova opened the door. Steven placed an immediate punch to his face. He slammed and continued to punch Casanova repeatedly before putting him in a chokehold.

"Steven, let him go!" Shai yelled, worried that he would kill Casanova. Where is Wren, Casanova?" She panicked, circling the room. Steven eased his chokehold a bit.

Casanova moved around, trying to free himself from Steven. "She is downstairs in her lab. What is going on? Why are you tripping, man?" He asked between breaths.

Shai ran to the lab to find Wren, who met her on the stairway. Wren was puzzled to see Shai. Within seconds she took off to the living room and met with

Casanova and Steven. Wren threw her arms in the air, landing them on her head. "Steven, what is going on? Let him go!"

Steven tightened his squeeze around Casanova's neck. "So, this dude has been beating you, sis?"

"Um, no, I mean, we disagree, but…." Wren struggled to tell the truth.

"Enough said!" Steven tightened his squeeze again, using all his strength. Casanova fought hard to gasp for air."

Wren moved in to help Casanova, grabbing Steven's hands to loosen his grip. "Steven, if you kill this man, you would be trading places with mom. Stop it! I cannot lose you." She begged her brother.

Steven loosened his grip, throwing Casanova off, causing Wren to fall with him. Steven helped Wren up from the floor, keeping his eyes on Casanova. Casanova remained frozen on the floor. Not sure if he had permission to move.

"Casanova, you got thirty minutes to pack whatever you need and get out of my sister's house. We will have the police here in minutes if you attempt to pull anything. I am sure they would love to see my sister's face." Steven threatened, taking a seat on a nearby couch. He pulled a gun from his pants pocket as Shai sat beside him.

"I agree with my brother, Casanova. I need you to go and go now!" Wren added.

Casanova got up slowly, keeping his eyes on Steven. He wanted to talk to Wren, but he knew it would be pointless with Steven. He quickly filled a suitcase with items and a few duffle bags inside their bedroom. He would call for their house cleaner the next day to pack more of his belongings and bring them back to the Hinsdale home. Casanova concluded that divorce was sure to follow, and the best thing to do from here was to follow suit and leave.

The next evening, Wren, Cartel, Jamie, and Garcia met at a local park for a walk. The ladies committed to getting back in shape together and finding ways to stay connected in their busy lives. It was a mid-forties winter day. Sunny enough for a walk but chilly enough to make it quick. They formed a unique sisterhood. A haven where they could laugh, joke and cry if needed. Wren had on a pair of dark sunglasses; not only did Casanova give her a nosebleed, but he also blackened her eye. Gratefully, the swollenness in her lip subsided to the point a little lipstick could hide.

"Ok, ladies, I will walk for only ½ mile and sit down. This is my first pregnancy, so I want to be as careful as possible." Jamie announced as they began the walking trail.

"Girl, we gotcha. It will be dark by 6 pm, so we cannot get in too many miles anyway." Cartel added.

"What is up the glasses, Wren? You remind me of the days when I had to wear dark glasses to hide my abuse from you all." Garcia asked, glancing at her.

"No, I am not hiding anything. My eyes are irritated today. I want to protect them as much as I can." Of course, Wren lied to protect her image. The women looked up to her success, and to learn she was in an abusive relationship would change their perspective.

"So, ladies, I also asked you all to meet here today because my cousin, Dr. Liza Littlejohn, is supposed to be meeting this dude she had been dating on an app today." Cartel told them.

"Wait, I thought she was supposed to meet him a few weeks ago, after my doctor's appointment?" Garcia asked. She recalled Cartel mentioning this to her during the car ride home.

"You are right, but he did not show. Or, she did not see him, I guess. So, they are meeting near that fountain over there for the first time. There she is by the fountain; let us sit on the bench across from it for a moment. She wanted me to be here in case something fishy came about. I do not want us to look suspicious."

They sat on the bench and continued to chat as the norm. Within minutes, a six-foot-older Black man with a medium-built, nice muscle frame and a salt and pepper low trimmed beard approached Liza at the fountain. He reached out to formally introduce himself as Henry Stallings, the man Liza previously mentioned. Liza was unhappy with Henry's appearance. She watched, not willing to shake his hand. After partaking in a moment of silence for a minute or two, she told him. "OMG, this is so bad. You cannot be the man I have been admiring for three months. You are Black!"

He responded, "I am Henry Stallings, the man you have spoken to daily over the last three months. You look amazing. Can we walk and talk?"

"No, I am sorry. This is a huge mistake. I do not date Black men. I could never." Liza retorted, walking away from Henry. She met eyes with her cousin, Cartel, shrugging her shoulders in disbelief.

Cartel stood up from the bench. She knew thoughts flooded Liza's head. "Liza!" she called out to her.

Ignoring her, Liza walked back to her car. *How did I miss the fact that he was black? So, the Black man in the restaurant was him the first time. We did not miss each other; I just missed the memo. Henry does not sound like a Black man on the phone. He had no slang,*

and his conversations were intelligent. His upbringing
seemed normal; how could I not detect this sooner?

"That was mean for your cousin to just walk away from dude like that," Jamie mentioned. She stood next to Cartel, shaking her head.

"Oh, I agree that was cold," Cartel said, watching Henry take off in the opposite direction. He looked a little embarrassed by his facial expressions. I feel bad for him."

"She sounds prejudiced, telling him she does not date black," Garcia added, joining them.

Wren got up to join them as well. Cartel watched Liza get back safely in her car and drive off. "I don't know what to do about her at times." She said, shaking her head.

The ladies began to walk a nearby trail, chattering about the situation. And although they all thought Henry was a nice-looking Black man, it would take hell to freeze over for Liza to see it.

On Thursday, Wren woke up in an unfamiliar setting. "Wren Davidson? I am Dr. Garza. Do you know where you are at this Thursday evening?"

"Yes, in a hospital, correct?" Wren asked, looking around the room. "Why am I here, though?"

"Well, I was hoping you could tell me that. Do you recall speaking to me in my office? We had an appointment to sit down and discuss something concerning you. During that time, you shared with me abuse you felt was happening inside your home or head?"

"I think so, but how did I get here?"

"Well, you appeared before me extremely high off something. Your pupils alerted me, and after two or three sentences, you began to lose consciousness. In your purse, I found the empty bottle. Thank goodness you came to a clinic staffed with therapists and medical doctors. We were able to aid you in using medication to counter the effects of opioid digestion."

"Why, did you save me? Dr. Garza, now things will only get worse."

"That is why I am here. I want to help you with whatever you are trying to escape. I cannot help you if you do not tell me."

Wren began to tear up. She battled with opening to folks. She pondered a moment. *If Casanova learned about the popping of pills, he would have more reasons to belittle me.* It felt as if he found joy in degrading, whipping, and making me feel useless. Leaving this world was the best means of escape. "I am not in an abusive relationship. I made it all up, Dr. Garza."

"Ok, can you share why you made it up?' Dr. Garza understood that abused women often took back their concerns out of fear.

"No, I want to go home. Can I go home now?"

"Well, we want to keep you here a day or two. Let your body rest a little bit. We want to make sure you are stable to go home."

"Did you call my husband by chance?"

"We have not called anyone now. However, we do have your next of kin as Steven Davidson. Is it ok that we call him?"

"Never, please do not alert him. My brother is a worrier, and this news would not be good for him. If you must call someone, please call Cartel Markham. She is the only person I trust to know this information." Wren jotted down her phone number and gave it to the doctor.

"Will do. You get to rest for now. I will be back to check on you in the AM. And Wren, you are safe here. No one is going to visit you or call you. We locked up all your personal belongings. We want you to rest worry-free. Ok?"

"Yes, and thank you," Wren responded, still concerned about Casanova's thoughts if he found out.

While adding the final changes to Jamie's hair at the salon, Cartel's phone rang. "Hello, this is Cartel; how can I help you?"

"Hi Cartel, your friend, Wren Davidson-Bryant, asked me to call you. She wanted you to know that she is fine and would be unavailable for a few days to rest."

"To rest, to rest, where?" Cartel asked.

"She is an inpatient at a local hospital. She is in excellent health. However, she requests no visitors and no phone calls. She will call you in a few days."

"Wait, this sounds like some program. Listen, I work with all types of broken women. I know this type of communication all too well. Please tell me where my friend is and who I can contact about her."

"Sure, you can contact me at any time. Would you please jot down my phone number 312-606-XXXX? I am Dr. Garza."

"Dr. Mandy Garza, the psychiatrist?" Cartel questioned.

"Yes, ma'am, and you're an evangelist, correct?"

"I am. I thought I knew your voice. We have met on a few occasions. Thank you for the call, and please take care of my friend. I will be praying for her." Cartel hung up the phone. She immediately began to blame herself. Wren struggled in her marriage to Casanova, and she knew it. Now, Wren is institutionalized, and it crushed her to think about it.

"Is everything ok?" Jamie asked, watching Cartel's eyes water.

"No, but all will be. I am going to head over to the barber side of the salon. I need to talk to my husband for a second." Cartel mentioned, quickly disappearing.

"George! Cartel yelled, running up to him. "I need to speak to you in private."

George excused himself from the client in his chair. "Babe, what's up?" he asked, pulling Cartel into a small closet room, shutting the door behind them.

Cartel, now shedding tears, slapped her hand across her forehead. Mad at herself for letting Wren down. "George, Wren told me several months ago that Casanova was abusing her. I would have mentioned it to you, but she changed her mind. She told me the abuse was not real."

"Wait, what?" George asked. He pulled Cartel close to him. "Start again? Where is Wren? What is going on?"

"Wren is in an inpatient unit under the care of a psychiatrist. My friend is not in a good space. I failed her. She told Jamie and me about this while joking around more than once. Then, bae, she flipped it to say, girl, we only play fight, or he is lightweight. So, I figured she would not play that way if it were real abuse."

George hugged her tight. "We are going to get through it. At least she is in a place she cannot harm herself right now. She needs time to think and rest. In the meantime, calm down and understand this is not your fault. God is in control here. We must trust him. And, I must find that punk, Casanova," George added, now fumed. "Wren is like a sister to me."

"No, George, you are right to trust God. I am tripping. I should go back in there and tell Jamie. I just walked out on the poor girl. If I know her well, she is still waiting for an explanation."

"Well, do not make it your business to tell her Wren's business. Friend or not. Let Wren be the one to let her know. Ok, my wife, my beautiful queen."

"Certainly, I would not do that anyway, especially not to Wren." Cartel opened the closet door, feeling much better about the situation. Knowing that God was in control and with that, Wren would be fine. Exiting the closet, a woman approached George and her. She looked upset.

"So, are you finally going to tell her, or should I?" the brown-skinned woman stood with a curly black ponytail. She wore an oversized brown shirt that coordinated well with her white leggings—staring at George with a nasty frown. Cartel, now confused, also looked to George.

"Trisha, this is not the time for your foolishness." George snapped at her.

"I am sorry, am I missing something here? Hi Trisha, I am his wife, Cartel. You appear flustered about something. Can I help you?"

"Aww, you are so cute. The little wifey wants to have her husband's back. I love it!" Trisha teased with a round of applause.

"No, seriously, can I help you?" Cartel repeated.

"Listen, this will be hard for you, pooh bear, but I cannot go on like this another day." Trisha began.

"Trisha, let me talk to my wife first and alone. Stop this foolishness now." George interrupted her.

"Too late. Mrs. Markham, I have your husband's baby. We are eight months pregnant. I was supposed to be silent until he built the strength to tell you himself. But I see that he needs my help. He has known about our child for over five months. You need to know about this child too."

"Wait, wait, wait a minute. As my husband said, move away from us with this foolishness. George would not cheat on me. George, she is making this whole thing up, correct?"

George stood silent. To see his wife stand by him in total belief that he would not hurt her saddened him. Now regretting the day, he got drunk. He was careless that night and in his feelings. Cartel had just miscarried for the third time. His spirit was weak, and he allowed the enemy to win. And although he prayed for forgiveness, the day Trisha called him with the pregnancy news thrilled him. Only he had wished it were Cartel.

"It is factual," Trisha responded. The day you lost your baby, he came to the club and found me. I was the woman who listened to him pour his heart out. He wanted a child so badly. He could not understand why you kept losing his seed." Trisha smiled, rubbing her stomach.

"And let me guess, you were there for him. You had sex with him and got pregnant on the first attempt. Lucky you!" Cartel responded sarcastically, "thanks for your support, George. I guess I had just too much faith in you." She walked away from them. Two negative disappointments in one hour were too much.

"Cartel!" George yelled out to her. "It is not what you think, bae!"

"She does not want to hear from you. You hurt her, and you are such a punk! Why did you sit there in silence like that?" Trisha added, shaking her head at him.

"I hate the day I met you. I truly do. I know the devil sent you to wreck a good Christian marriage, but you and the devil will not gain victory here. I love my wife. I am not leaving her. She and I will get through this, and I pray that is not my baby." George snapped, walking away from her.

Friday evening, Garcia, Jamie, and Cartel met up for dinner. After ordering their meals and drinks, Cartel began updating the ladies about Wren. She kept details minimal, advising her friends; Wren went away for a few days. She needed time to clear her head.

"Hey, I understand having time alone is essential," Garcia responded, taking a sip of water from a glass.

"So, will you tell me why you rushed out of the salon yesterday? I know you got that phone call and ran to speak to George, but what? You just rushed right past me and left the salon. We are not as close as Wren and me, but I consider you a sister." Jamie asked Cartel.

"Jamie, I needed to wrap my head around something, that's all."

"I saw that much, but are you better today? I mean, do you need to talk? I tried calling you last night, no answer. I tried calling Wren, but now I know why she did not answer."

"I am in deep prayer these days. Talking about it will not help until I get an understanding. I am lost now, but I must stand strong and trust God."

"You can stand firm in faith and still talk to your friends, Cartel. Holding all that stuff inside will drive you insane. You take on everyone's issues and pray for so many people. Why would you not allow people to do the same for you?" Jamie asked.

"I know you got my best interest at heart, Jamie, but I need more time. However, I do wish I could call Wren right now. You two are also my sisters, but this is too personal. I am not ready to discuss it." Cartel teared up.

"Cartel, I have never seen you this jittery before; it makes me so nervous," Garcia added, grabbing her friend's hand. "You've been there for me; let me help you now."

"Listen, we are supposed to be enjoying our evening out laughing and joking. I do not want to feel down. Could we please talk about something else?" Cartel begged, taking a napkin to wipe her face.

"Well, I have some good news. I am going to marry Yesenia once my divorce finalizes from Jose." Garcia shared, grinning from ear to ear.

"I am so happy for you, friend!" Jamie said, sending a silent clap from across the table.

"And you, Cartel? Are you happy for me?" Garcia looked over at her.

"I cannot say that I am happy about your decision to marry another woman, but I can say that I am happy; you are happy."

"That is some bull Cartel! I can never get a straight answer out of you regarding my situation. Why is it so hard for you to accept it?"

"Really, Garcia? You want to go there today, out of all days?"

"No, she doesn't." Jamie pleaded, whispering, *stop it* to Garcia.

"Garcia, just know I love you and always will, little sis!" Cartel added.

"Yep, I can definitely feel the love, Cartel," Garcia responded, shaking her head.

"Well, Cartel, if you do not want to allow us to help you. I would love to share something concerning me. Can I share?" Jamie asked.

"Of course, you can share your concerns, Jamie. I am always here for my friends no matter what I go through."

"Well, my sister, Kimmel, is acting strange around me lately. Since we shared the news about my pregnancy, she has been making comments and picking fights with me."

"Really, well, she thinks her son, Jordan, will get less attention from you and Karl now. I cannot see another reason for her to be jealous or start acting out."

"I was thinking the same thing. She is acting strange. It has gotten to the point where I asked her to find her a place."

"It is that bad? How so?" Cartel asked.

"She asked Karl if he would show favoritism towards his new baby and just leave Jordan behind. He told her he would never do that."

"Yep, sounds like jealousy," Garcia confirmed.

Exactly, and my husband looked highly uncomfortable when she asked that. I told her enough was enough. She was already commenting on how dramatic I had been acting over my pregnancy. Weird, so we agreed that she needs to move out."

The server brought out their meals. After grace, they jumped right into their plates. The sound of lips smacking and finger-licking from all three women meant excellent food. As Cartel focused on her food, she silently prayed for words to say regarding Jamie's situation. Jamie had been taking care of her siblings for years. And although Kimmel is an adult, pushing her out might damage their sibling bond. Having Kimmel stay could hurt her marriage, so the situation had to get treated with care.

The server returned. "Is there anything else I can get for you, ladies?"

"We are good, thank you!' Cartel responded, taking another bite of her food.

"Ok, Cartel. Something is off with you. You are not a good friend right now." Jamie brought it out. "The silence is not you by far."

"Forgive me, please. I try not to speak out of turn. I try to say less if the Lord does not give me anything. The truth is, I am not sure why Kimmel is acting out suddenly. But I find peace in thinking it relates to Jordan."

"For sure, and I know that Karl and I need to discuss it with her before she leaves that Jordan will always be a priority in our lives."

"And with that, all should work out just fine." Cartel half-smiled at her. Advising others was natural for her. If only her current situation were that easy, she thought—a message populated across her cell phone. She reached for it on the table. It was Casanova, asking her if Wren was with her. She responded, *no, but she is okay.* Also, there were three missed calls and eight text messages from George. Cartel did not go home last night; she slept at a hotel. She had no energy to speak to

George. She waived to the waiter to bring their check and some containers.

"What is your problem, Cartel, for real?" Garcia asked. "I have been watching you this evening, and something is wrong. And now you are calling for a check already?"

"For the last time, I will tell you both when the time is right. Something is wrong, but I have nothing to share until I find the truth. I cannot share what I do not know or understand now."

"Well, that is fair. You should take your time and be comfortable when talking about heart matters. The wrong timing or advice could make things worse." Jamie agreed.

"My point exactly, and ladies, I will take care of the check. I appreciate you for just spending time with me this evening." Cartel told them. She received the check from the server as he handed them to-go containers.

"No appreciation needed; that's what friends are for, I thought," Garcia provided a delayed response, shrugging her shoulders at Jamie. She was starting to get annoyed with Cartel. If Cartel did not feel comfortable speaking to them about her problems, was there a friendship?

Casanova sent another message to Cartel asking if he could come to her house and speak to George and her this evening. She stared at her phone, unsure how to respond. She and George were not in a good place for any company. Plus, she had not seen George since she left the shop yesterday. She pondered. *Then again, having Casanova over could stall the conversation needed between George and her*. Cartel wrote back. *Sure, see you at about 8 pm*, regardless of whether George was home. Whenever he got home, he would never speak about the infidelity in front of Casanova. "Well, sisters, I am going to head home now. This has been great! And let us do this again soon when Wren's back." Cartel added, jumping up from the table.

"Yep, I am all for it. And thanks again for the food." Jamie agreed, joining her on her feet. Cartel gave both ladies a quick hug and went about her way.

"Are you good, Garcia?" Jamie asked, detecting unhappiness.

"Yes, and no, I don't like how she withholds her affairs but is quick to advise others regarding their concerns or pitfalls."

"Hey, it is all good. I understand her. Wren is her best friend. She needs her. I am only glad to know them both." Jamie responded, giving Garcia a light hug. "See you next time."

Cartel opened the front door for Casanova. He followed her into the den where George was watching television. George had no idea Casanova was coming over. Nor did he realize his wife had gotten home. Cartel had purposely avoided him; she had taken a shower, put on lounging clothes, and never spoke to him. George turned off the television. He looked at Cartel, then to Casanova. "You good, man?" he questioned.

"Yeah, man. I just came over to talk with you and Cartel for a minute or two. I have things I need to get off my chest."

"That is cool. Have a seat, dawg." George looked at Cartel again. He wanted to speak to her but knew she was unwilling to talk.

Casanova took a seat on the couch next to George. Cartel sat directly across from them in a chair. She kept her eyes on Casanova, fighting hard not to see George. Casanova looked at both. It was like he felt the tension in the air. "Is this a suitable time?" he then asked.

"Yep, all is well. How can we help you?" Cartel responded, trying to avoid further delay.

"Well, I started seeing a marriage counselor. I have made mistakes in my marriage that may have caused Wren to leave me." Casanova began.

"Interesting; how so? What kind of mistakes, Casanova?" Cartel asked him.

"Well, I have put my hands on her two times. And I am not happy about that. I struggle with getting her to trust me, listen to me, acknowledge that I am the head, and know I got us. She is a bulldog, and it is hard to walk in unison with a woman like that."

Cartel giggled and shook her head. Her friend was a bulldog, as in strong, but placing his hands on her was no excuse. "Pardon, my giggle. I agree that my friend can be difficult to reason with, but the abuse is inexcusable."

"You are correct; I agree. I am not sure where the abuse is coming from, Cartel. Before her, I never hit a woman. I struggle with understanding why I snap when it comes to her."

"Could it be that you went into marriage with your expectations? I have read that when people enter marriage with their allusions, it is a recipe for disaster."

"I won't say that I came with full expectations of how my marriage should flow, but I came from a good household, so there might've been some influences."

"I think so. Casanova, you are a great man. I know you love my friend, Wren. I also know that your mother, Anna, loves you. She is a piece of work, as you can agree. But what worked for your parent's marriage might not work for yours."

"I agree, Cartel. I have come to that realization. After my session this morning, I went to my parents and said the same thing. They know that I have run my wife away. I cannot say that my mother was sad because she was not. Yet, my father made the same statement as you. I must be the man of my castle. I cannot follow him in all things."

"Did your father ever hit your mother in your presence?" George asked, breaking his silence.

"Funny you would ask that. That was part of my reason for visiting them as well. In front of my mother, I asked him if he had ever hit her before. And the answer was no."

"More interesting," Cartel responded. "So, your actions are not learned behavior; it is something that lies in you, bro. You must figure out where it stimulates. Some men struggle with women rejecting their thoughts and plans for the family. Some men want a woman who agrees with everything and has no voice. You have to let God lead from this point. God was not part of your decision when you chose Wren to be your wife. If my thoughts are correct, your marriage did not start on the right grounds. Your peace now interrupted."

"That is deep, Cartel. That is real talk. I do not believe I allowed God to lead me in my decision to marry Wren. I let the wrong head lead me. She was the finest chick I ever met. I loved her grind and that she did not need me for anything. She matched all my expectations, her intelligence and all. So, I ran with it. I never even thought to pray to God about her."

"And you know what, bro, I applaud you for being honest. Wren is all of that and more. She might have been what God has for you, but not at that time. There are levels to everything. Moving before the Lord can also lead us down the wrong path."

"So, now what do I do? " He asked.

"What do you want to do?" Cartel responded with a question.

"I want my marriage to work. I do love Wren. I need to learn how to treat her. I regret all the harsh words I said to her, but I do not know how to fix it, Cartel."

"That is an excellent place to start, Casanova. Knowing that you love her is all that is needed right now. Wren is somewhere having the much-needed time to herself. You both need this peace break to sort things out. You cannot fix this without God's help. But, if you both are determined to stay married, you will win. Start by asking God to forgive you."

"I have asked him to forgive me for abusing my wife." Casanova shared.

"And ask him to forgive you for moving too fast in this marriage. If Wren was not the wife he had for you, ask him to forgive you for that too. Ask him to show you how to receive her if she is the wife. That is the best advice I have for you now. You must let him lead. You must keep the vows now that you are in the marriage."

"That's good advice, and I appreciate you for that," Casanova responded, feeling a sense of relief that he was able to come clean about his actions and find support in rebuilding his union with Wren.

"Do you think there is any hope for us?" George asked, looking at Cartel.

"Hold up, are you good? I feel something in the air. You two are normally loved up in a corner somewhere." Casanova asked George.

"Man, you are not the only one messing up these days. There is a woman named Trisha with whom I had made a horrible mistake. I slept with her. I think anyway. I was drunk and mad that Cartel kept miscarrying our babies. I allowed the devil to invade my thoughts that night. In my mind, I was leaving Cartel. I was tired of not having any children. Yet, when the liquor wore off, I was not proud of my thoughts that led to those actions."

"Oh wow!" Casanova responded. He glanced at Cartel, "Cartel, I am sorry you must be hurting from all that is happening. I did not mean to come here and add to it. And, George, I do not have any words, man. The devil is busy wrecking marriages. Anything of God, he attacks. Just stay a prayerful man." George responded to Casanova with a half-smile.

"Thank you, Casanova. And no worries! I am always here for you and Wren." Cartel told him. "I am going to leave you two now. It is my bedtime. I have a busy schedule in the AM."

The following day, Wren got released from the hospital. Staff determined she was not a suicide threat and that outpatient treatment suited her. She decided to call Casanova: she missed him and knew he had to be worried about her disappearance.

He picked up, "Wren, hey, I miss you. Where are you?"

"I just got released from a mental institution. I am not sure how I got there, but it was something to do with us."

"A mental institution, how embarrassing is that? Do they know you are married to me?"

"Typical Casanova, more concerned about his reputation than his wife," Wren responded, nodding her head back and forth.

"No, baby, do not think of it that way. I do care about you, but I am a well-known actor. We do not need that type of publicity."

Casanova always said the right words to trigger a negative response from Wren. She sat quietly on the phone, driving and deeply thinking—another thing to add to his insult list. Casanova went on and on. He became aggravated at her silence and began to yell through the phone.

"I don't know why I keep thinking this will work with you." Wren finally responded, having heard enough of his rants.

"Yeah, same here! You are going to ruin my career. What happened to all your intelligence? You are stupid; who would admit themselves into a mental institution? Do you know who your husband is?" Casanova continued.

"Casanova, I am tired of defending myself. You should start the divorce process if you can no longer see my worth. Here I am, hating myself. For what?" she yelled back at him.

"Well, you should hate yourself. I knew better than to marry a girl from the hood. What was I thinking? My mother tried to warn me." He added.

Broken7

Wren listened as Casanova continued to take jabs at her. Tears flowed from her eyes. *How did I get to this point where a man's words paralyzed me?* She thought to herself, not paying attention to the traffic lights. The sounds of screeching brake pads and wheels came through the phone.

"Wren! Casanova yelled through the phone. Are you ok? 'He could hear Wren screaming.

Moments later, the sounds of glass breaking and people yelling. Someone asked if Wren was ok. Casanova could not hear Wren anymore. He flipped open the cell phone tracker to ping her location. "I am on my way, baby! You are about five minutes away from your home. I will be there in a second!" he yelled. He dashed out the front door to his vehicle. He was praying and pleading the blood of Christ over his wife. He hoped to find his wife stable and alive.

George, Cartel, Casanova, Jamie, and Steven sat patiently for hours in the emergency room, awaiting Wren's update. The medical team discovered internal injuries and bleeding. Casanova continued to blame himself for causing the accident. Steven, not precisely sure what Casanova meant by his actions, jumped in his face several times. He threatened to kill him if anything happened to his sister due to his actions. The emergency room team warned the group. If one more outbreak occurred, everyone would have to leave the hospital.

"How is she doing?" a woman appeared before them, wearing all black. Her skin was dark chocolate, her hair as white as snow. She walked over to Casanova, "How is my daughter doing? I saw via television news she had a bad accident."

"I'm sorry, have we met before?" Casanova looked up at her. He knew Wren had an estranged relationship with her mother but had never seen her before.

Steven got up from his chair and walked over to him and Wren's mother, Sharon. "Mom, we have not gotten an update yet about her. She went down to surgery hours ago. They will let us know more in a bit.

"Wow! Ms. Davidson!" Casanova chimed in. "I am honored to meet you finally." Casanova stood and embraced her with a hug. Although he was glad to meet her, he was unsure how Wren would receive her presence.

"Thank you, Casanova. I do not know much about you. I have watched several of the movies you starred in, and I've been following your and Wren's social media pages. You treat my daughter well."

"Well, let us not assume that much, mom. He might have something to do with her being here. And if he does, he already knows what is coming for him." Steven threatened, guiding his mother to a seat next to him.

"Good to see you as always, Ms. Davidson." Cartel spoke as she sat between Steven and her.

"Thanks, Cartel. How are you?" she asked.

"I am hanging in there. Keeping my mind stayed on Christ. I know Wren is a fighter; she will be just fine."

"I agree. I have not seen my baby girl since she was a child. Lord knows this cannot be the end for her. While I was in the pen, I asked the Lord to get me through. Get me back to my children, and I will serve him for the rest of my life. And he did just that. Steven and I are reconnecting, so I know this is the Lord's doing. He had to sit my baby down and give her peace. So she could reconnect with her mother and grow closer to him."

"That is a terrific way to look at things, Ms. Davidson! It might be some truth to it. Although Wren does not believe in God, he still believes in her."

"Yes, he does. And I know God is working it out for her too. Now, I do not know what has been going on with her because, as you know, she will not talk to me. But God knows what she needs."

"Amen to that, Ms. Davidson! I am glad you have the courage to show up. Hopefully, Wren will light up when she sees you."

"I hope so. Now, how about you? How do you feel about the news you received?"

"Huh, how did you know about the infidelity?" Cartel questioned, turning to face her.

"Infidelity?" She questioned, now looking at George. So many words came to mind as their eyes met. It gave her a flashback of how her husband, Daniel, ran off with that woman and threw her children into the system. She hated men that cheated.

Tapping her on the shoulder to regain her attention, Cartel asked, "Ms. Davidson, what were you saying to me?"

"Baby girl, you have enough with your husband. Never mind what I was fixing to ask you. You have accepted that part of the news. But this here, with your husband, is enough to deal with. Then you got your best friend, fighting for her life. We will talk later."

"No, Ms. Davidson, I want to know. Please, what news?"

"Well, first, stop calling me Ms. Davidson. You are an adult, and it is acceptable to call me Sharon. And second, we can talk later. We got time."

"Mr. Bryant and the family of Wren Davidson-Bryant, please follow me to the family room to the left.

The doctor will be in to meet with you." A nurse informed, guiding the family to a private room.

Steven sat away from Casanova, fighting hard to stay calm as they waited for the doctor to arrive. Sharon and Cartel sat next to each other with grabbed hands. They quietly prayed in agreement, interceding for Wren. As for George and Jamie, they remained in the waiting room. Finally, the doctor and a chaplain entered the room.

"How is she?" Casanova jumped up from his chair, anxious to receive some news.

"She is stable but has a long road of recovery ahead of her. She suffered some internal bleeding and swelling in the brain. We lost her during the surgery, but we got her back. Unfortunately, she is in a coma, medically induced coma."

"What?!' Casanova yelled, falling to his knees. "God no, bring her back!"

"Stupid, he said she is back, just in a coma. Get up!" Steven yelled out, turning to the doctor. "Can we see her?"

"Not everyone at one time. One or two at a time. And not for long." The doctor responded.

"Thank you, doctor!" Cartel shook his hand.

"May I offer prayer for the family?" the chaplain asked.

"Thank you, but we are a praying family. We got this!" Sharon responded. "Now, Casanova, you need to get up from your knees. This moment is not the time for weeping. Whatever has happened is now in the past; get up and make it right. Go in there and see about your wife."

Casanova followed Wren's mother's instructions. The chaplain walked with him to Wren's room. Still upset with Casanova, Steven thought of ways to destroy him as he & the rest of the family moved back to the waiting room.

"So, Sharon, are you going to tell me now? I would like to know. And since all is well with Wren, I have room to receive whatever it is." Cartel restarted their conversation.

"You and Wren are a piece of work. I can see why you two became the best of friends. You don't leave well enough alone, do you?" Sharon said, delivering a twisted smile.

"Hey, we are strong; God knew we needed each other."

"Yes indeed. I was just wondering, well, I could use your advice. I know that you recently found out that Susan is your birth mother. So, I was hoping to gain some advice from you. How were you able to forgive her? How difficult was it for you to move forward? I am just trying to learn from you in hopes it could help Wren and me."

"Whoa! Sharon! Who is my birth mother? My parents died in a car accident when I was five years old. I think you have gotten me mixed up with someone else."

"Oh baby, I must have mixed you up with someone else. I do apologize. Susan told me that she had spoken to you. You know which Susan I am referring to, correct? Your client, Susan, is from the flower shop near your salon. She told me she was looking into reservations for a mom and daughter luncheon at the Hyatt. She made it seem like you two talked and were looking forward to building a relationship. I apologize again. I might have spoken out of turn."

George rosed from his chair, quickly moving closer to Cartel. The words that flew from Sharon's mouth brought his wife into a hollow state. He could tell her thoughts were all over the place. He reached for her hand. She moved it away from him. Cartel was unsure if what she heard Sharon say applied to her life. She thought Sharon must have mixed the story with someone else, shaking the news off.

Casanova re-entered the waiting room. His thoughts on Wren's condition differed from what the doctor had explained. The look on his face was enough for Cartel and Sharon to dart past him; they needed to see Wren. Casanova informed Jamie and George that he would be back in an hour or so. He was unwilling to leave his wife at that hospital alone, and he was only going home to shower and get clothes. They agreed to stay with Wren until he returned.

Bedtime at the Markham's house was still an awkward atmosphere. Cartel showered and laid close to her end of the bed. She barely spoke to George since the alleged affair. She hoped he had no energy to talk tonight. George climbed into the bed. He wrestled around, trying to find comfort. He knew Cartel needed him right now, but guilt consumed him. After a few more rolls around the bed, he decided to chat anyway. "Cartel! Are you sleeping yet?" He tapped her shoulder.

"No, I am not sleeping, just in deep thought." She responded.

"In deep thought about us, Wren, or the thought of Susan being your birth mother?"

"How about all three!" she answered, rising from the bed. Placing her back against the headboard, she looked at him.

He rosed up to join her. "I want you to be happy again. I am not too fond of your appearance lately. You are normally joyous; lately, all I see is pain."

"Well, thank you for the bulk of that pain. Then, not having my best friend's ear to listen does not help me deal with things either. And last, regarding Wren's mom, Sharon. I do not think her story is factual. Susan is not my mother; my parents died in a car accident. My birth certificate clearly shows my mother's name, matching the obituary from her funeral. I second guess her story, so I pulled out those boxes in the hallway. I had to make sure everything was clear."

"Yeah, I am not sure about Susan being your birth mother, but it is worth asking Susan. It would allow you to meet her real daughter and help them through whatever situation they are dealing with. You mentioned she has this daughter that she talks about, yet no one has ever seen."

"No, I have no more room to take on anyone else's battles. I have been praying and fighting for everyone else sanity. I need prayer warriors to uplift me right now. That hurt me to the core to hear that woman say you talked about me that way to her. Why didn't you say those things to me directly?"

"Say, what?" he asked, moving closer to her.

"Why did you not ask me why I kept losing our babies? That would have been the best thing to do. I could take it from you, better than her." Cartel lowered her head.

"I cannot even blame the liquor, bae. I was hurt that night. I could not understand why God would not bless us with our baby. I questioned God because we are faithful to him. We pray, try to live right, pay our tithes to a church, and give to charity. I was thinking of paying a surrogate to carry the baby. Then, I made the mistake of telling this to that whore at the club."

"No need to call her names now. She is carrying your unborn child." Cartel shook her head, saddened every time she thought about it.

"I am not confident that is my child, Cartel. I do not know that woman. If she slept with me that easy without protection, she could have slept with another man the night before."

"That is true, NASTY! And I thought you knew better than that!" Cartel snapped at him.

"I told you. My mind was in an altered state. I have no idea what went on that night. My memory is unclear. Now, I understand why the bible speaks about drunkenness. For me, it is better not to drink at all."

"Correct. Drunkenness will not inherit the kingdom. And Ewe…furthermore, that lady could have HIV or something. You better pray that is not so." she added, making a mental note to call her gynecologist for a check-up.

"I think if she had HIV, she would know by now. She is pregnant, and they do check for things like that."

"Right, they do. That does not mean she would tell you. You do not know her." Cartel snapped.

"You are correct to say that, but I trust God, all is well."

"Oh, you want to trust God on that part, but not that he would bless me to carry our baby to full term. Do not you dare put trusting God in your sin. I could hate you right now."

"But you do not. You love me, Cartel. And I love you. I made a mistake one time per that woman. And I promise I will never make that mistake again if you forgive me."

"Well, I must forgive you, but I do not have to stay in this marriage. You broke the vow, the covenant you made with me before the Lord. You slept with someone else, which is grounds for a divorce. I want you to file it; I want out of the mess. There is no way I could watch another woman bring forth your child with me on the sidelines, just smiling. Do you really think that is in me? No way!"

"Seriously! Just like that?" George got up from the bed. The thought of losing Cartel made him feel sick. "You will allow a female to make you leave your husband?"

"You sound like you do not understand what just happened here. You allowed some woman to take you from your wife. It was your actions with her that caused the division. I do not trust you anymore, so it will never work," Cartel explained. "I will call my lawyer in the morning." She rosed up from the bed to face him.

"No, we do not end it like this. Marriage is a lifetime commitment. We are not going to be part of the worldly statistics."

"You sound so much like a great man right now, but you are not! You are petty and sad. You are weak, and I am finished with you and this marriage."

"Cartel, you counsel many people to stay together, hang in, and finish the race. Yet, when it comes to matters of your heart, you quit. I do not even know if this baby is mine."

"What do you expect me to do, sir? Wait to see if this baby is yours. If it is, then what? Just watch you become a father to a child that is not mine. That is hard!" Cartel turned from him. She pulled a pillow off the bed; it was best for her to sleep elsewhere.

"Where are you going?" George asked.

"I am going to sleep in the guest room. I do not want to talk about this anymore. You do not lose here; I do. If this is your baby, you gain what you have wanted."

George's heart sunk as he watched Cartel leave him alone. He regretted his actions from that night. He prayed that the baby was not his and that he could win his wife back. One part of him understood the strength Cartel would need to watch him raise a child with another woman. If the shoe were on the other foot, he was unsure if he could stay with her. Yet another part of him wanted Cartel to find that strength. She was his best friend. His life would not be complete without her. Starting over with another woman was not an option. He wanted his wife. He turned over to pray. God was the only one who could help them.

Tuesday morning, the salon was busy; it almost felt like the weekend. The AM flew by, and Cartel never stopped to eat breakfast or lunch. George had a bouquet of roses delivered to the shop. He asked Susan to stop by and give them to Cartel. He wanted Susan to clear things up with Cartel and resolve the unknown.

"Special delivery for you, my dear," Susan said, approaching Cartel's hair station.

"Thank you, Ms. Susan. How are you today?" Cartel asked, taking the roses from her. The scent was lovely, and the thought improved her day.

"I am well; how are you? Susan responded.

"I am well, thanks for asking. So, why are you delivering roses? You have a delivery person down there."

"I know I do, but I always bring things down here, so why not today."

"Understandable. Well, I know these roses are not part of your normal routine, and it looks like a card is inside. I can only assume where they came from." Cartel half-smiled, placing the roses on the table.

"Yep, you assumed correctly. Your husband is a great man. He loves you. Is this a suitable time to talk? I see that no one is in your chair right now, but it looks busy here. Do you have a moment?" Susan asked.

"I do, especially for you. Follow me to the backroom, please." Cartel responded, motioning for Susan to follow.

They sat at a small table in what could be a small break room. Cartel stared across the table at Susan. She looked for any resemblance and found none. *This woman is not my mother*, she thought. Cartel knew Susan had a daughter out there, and now was the best time for her to elaborate about why she would tell folks she was her daughter.

"Ok, Cartel, this is awkward. You are staring at me. And I am not sure why."

"Well, you mentioned you wanted to talk, so here I am."

"Let us get right to it. I believe I have confirmed evidence that I am your birth mother. Also, I have known where you were all of your life."

"Ms. Susan, this does not make any sense. My parents are deceased. You mentioned you have a daughter, but I am not her. I thought you had a relationship with your daughter, anyway?"

"I do. I was referring to the relationship that I have with you. I apologize for not being there for you. I have been trying to bond with you and compensate for the lost time."

"Help me make sense of this, Ms. Susan. Why do you think I am your daughter?"

"You mean, how do I know you are my daughter?" Susan responded, pulling out a birth record. She handed it to Cartel.

After reading it thoroughly, Cartel exclaimed. "Um, a birth record, paperwork filled out to prepare a birth certificate. How did you know my dad? I see his name and your name, but this is not making sense. I need you to be transparent. And NOW!" Cartel's voice sharpened, sliding the paperwork towards her on the table. *How dare this woman bring a wrinkled birth record to me as proof? This must be a joke*, she thought.

"Please allow me to explain. My father was the head Pastor of one of the largest churches in Chicagoland. It would have ruined my father's career if the congregation found out I had gotten pregnant out of wedlock by your father, Jesse. So, my mother and I hid the pregnancy from my father. I had an ill aunt, so it made sense to live with her and help. She was my mother's sister, so it just all worked out. Your father was adamant about giving him full custody of you and your grandmother; his mother was willing to help raise you. Instead of putting you up for adoption, I gave your father full custody as he demanded."

"So, you were in a relationship with my father? When was that? He was with my mother, Trina."

"No, your father and I never dated, but we occasionally met up; that is how I got pregnant with you. He was a big-time drug dealer with loads of money and nice cars. I admired street guys. I have always admired black men regardless of whether they were street or book intelligent. He later got involved with Trina when I was about six months pregnant with you. They got married not even one week after you were born. She became the mother you knew until she was killed in an auto accident. Well, until they had a bad drug deal."

"Lord, please tell me this woman is not telling the truth," Cartel said aloud. All she wanted to believe was what she got told all her life. Her parents, Jesse and Trina Tombs, had died when she was young. She did not want to believe anything different. "So, why did you allow my grandmother to keep me after my parents died? Or, better yet, once my grandmother passed, why did you allow me to go into the system?"

Susan shook her head. "Listen, I asked your grandmother if I could see you once or twice, and I was denied those visits. She told me you were too young to get confused by all the information you would uncover. And, I agreed, she was right."

"So, why would you let me go into foster care? You have tracked me all my life. After my grandma died, why didn't you come for me?"

"I have no answer. I just did not. And that is why I beat myself up so badly."

"That answer is not acceptable. Why come for me now? You do realize that I am almost forty years old. I do not need a relationship with you this late in life."

"Because my life was so incomplete without you. I had to make things right."

"Make things right, huh? Well, you have no idea what I have been through in life. Understand this, MOTHER. I got raped in foster care by a foster parent and became pregnant by him. My foster mother, instead of helping me, punished me. She took me to have an abortion at some cheap ghetto clinic. I do not even think the providers were licensed, clinicians. The sexual trauma and other traumatic abuse in my life led to post-traumatic syndrome disorder. Today, I am still suffering. I feel I cannot have children or carry a child to full term because of my foster care experiences. The news of others successfully carrying babies angers me. Do you want to know more?"

"No, because I am not good at coping, especially with that type of information, Cartel. I do not want to think about the past. You are successful. God has brought you through."

"Yes, God has. I do not know what you expect from me today. I have no room for you if you want a relationship with me. My life is a total mess right now. My best friend, the only person who genuinely cares about me, is fighting for her life. My husband is having a baby with another woman. And now, my so-called natural mother decides to show up with her truth. I cannot deal with all of this. I allowed you to speak your peace. I hope that made you feel better as a woman, a pathetic woman—one who cared more about her father's reputation than her unborn child. I pray you have mistaken me as your daughter. So far, I see that I am nothing like you!!!"

"Understandable, and I am sorry. I do want to ask one more thing before I leave."

"Sure, what?" Cartel asked, getting up from her chair.

"Does your husband know about your childhood trauma? If he does not, he needs to know. And, if I could give you one piece of advice. Many women in this salon admire what you and George have built together. They want your life. George told me about the woman carrying his seed. Fight for your marriage. Many miserable women are preying, and I do not mean praying for their own man like George. It is your great man they seek. I am leaving now. If you ever decide you want to speak to me, I am right down the street."

Cartel exhaled for a moment taking in all that Susan said. She knew many women admired her marriage to George. She also knew that George was one in a million, a great catch. But currently, she was not in a place to trust him. Without trust, the relationship would not survive. Although her advice was great, having Susan leave was the best for both.

"Cartel returned to the salon motioning for the next client to sit in her chair.

George walked up. How did that go?" he asked, watching Susan leave the salon.

"Why did you send her here? Why did you have her deliver those flowers? Did she tell you also that she is my birth mother?" Cartel asked as her client sat in her chair.

"Yes, she told me. I asked her about it when I purchased the roses. I told her what Sharon told you at the hospital. She confirmed that Sharon's thoughts were accurate."

"So, you thought having her deliver the flowers would allow us an opportunity to discuss it and hug and be the best of friends, correct?"

"Bae, you always said you would give anything to have your mother back in your life. How many times have you said that to Wren and me? You and my mother are so close, but even she cannot fill that void. Then to learn your mother is alive and well. Why wouldn't I try?"

"Trina! Trina was my mother. Trina is not alive and well. She died when I was five years old, remember? Let us not change the narrative. I would give anything to see Trina again! That Susan woman confirmed that Trina had been in my life since birth. I will not allow Susan to change my life. My parents are deceased. My grandma Lean is the other person I mourn. Not this Susan lady. But it all makes sense now."

"What makes sense?" George asked.

"My dad, his family loves me. However, my mother's family treats me differently. I bet my cousin Liza knew we were not first cousins. I bet she knows her Aunt Trina never had any children. It all makes sense now. I am going to speak to Liza about it. She is the only person I trust to confirm this information."

"Cartel, your cousin Liza is not the best source of truth. She might have some information, but the way she talks badly about us Black people, she might not be the best person to confide in about this."

"Do you want to speak to your husband in private?" the lady in the chair interrupted: I feel uncomfortable listening to all of this."

"No, it is fine, Lexi! At this point, the world already knows my business anyway."

"Yeah, you are right; you have been the latest gossip lately. But for what it is worth, you do resemble Ms. Susan. And I know it might be hard to digest all of this, but if you honestly believe in God, you talk all your clients' heads off about it. This situation would be a time for you to practice what you teach. Do not just cancel that woman out of your life. Now, I will be quiet." Lexi added, placing her earphones in her ears.

Cartel shrugged and rolled her eyes at Lexi, still focusing on George. "Listen, Liza is a difficult breed, but it is her or no one. The rest of them are stale and uneasy about communicating at times."

"Let me go with you, at least. I want to be there as support." George asked.

"No, I am still not sure about you either. If I were not a Christian, I could easily hate everyone right now.

"You should not speak that way. It would be best if you did not talk about hating folks. I understand you are disappointed in me, but love is still present. I understand Susan hit you with a heap of anonymous information, and I am not asking you to accept it. Do not speak to hating folks because life in your eyes is a vision of disappointment right now. You are better than that, Cartel!" George encouraged.

"Valerie, can you finish Lexi's hair for me? I need to get out of here." Cartel yelled out to another hairstylist.

"I sure will, right after I rinse my client," Valerie responded from across the room.

"Are you cool with that, Lexi?" Cartel asked, grabbing her things to leave.

"I am cool. Valerie does hair well." Lexi replied, shrugging her shoulders.

"Thank you. I am going to comp your expenses today. Free on me, Lexi! Have a great afternoon." Cartel explained, leaving the salon.

Chapter Four: It Aint Over

It had been two weeks since Wren went into the hospital. Casanova excitedly called Cartel's phone to confirm Wren's awakening earlier that morning. After praying and reading scriptures with Casanova, Wren asked about Cartel. Cartel raced to the hospital to see her friend. She learned the doctors updated her to good condition and said she could go home in a few days after careful monitoring and testing.

Cartel gave Wren the longest hug. Tears of joy streamed down her face. "I missed you, sister. So much has happened in my life while you rested."

"So much has happened in my life as well, Cartel. Casanova, could you please allow me time to talk with Cartel? I want to tell her what the Lord laid on my heart for her."

"Wait, what? The Lord? Casanova, did I hear this woman mention the Lord?"

"Yes, you did. For the last two weeks, I have been going to therapy and coming to the hospital to be here with my wife. I have been praying over her and asking the Lord to bring her back to us with her heart, mind, and soul opened to him." Casanova began.

"Well, we've all done that much, Casanova." Cartel responded.

"No, but there is more. I will allow my wife to tell you about her experience. I will check back on you two in about an hour."

"Sounds good. Now, first, what God are you talking about?" Cartel asked, sitting in a chair next to Wren's hospital bed.

"The God of Israel. The God of Abraham, Issac, and Jacob, Yah. The father of Christ Jesus, Yeshua. As I rested in this hospital bed, I got a vision clear as day. Beforehand, I struggled to understand the King James Version of the Bible. I wondered who the peculiar people were and where those people's descendants were today. One thing became evident, and that is who we are. We are a peculiar people. This morning, I asked Casanova to read **Deuteronomy 14.** Included in that chapter is a verse that says, *"For thou art, a holy people unto the Lord thy God, and the Lord hath chosen thee to be a peculiar people unto himself, above all the* *nations that are upon the earth."* Things are starting to make sense, but there is still much to uncover. I am ready to learn all that I can. The privileged people of this world have done an excellent job erasing our history. The Bible says that knowledge shall increase in the last days. I have read that in Daniel, chapter 12 but never entirely understood it!"

"But God! Wow!" Cartel said. She awaited the day her friend would come to her senses about Christ. And although she was not sure about being part of the bloodline, she was glad to know that her friend awakened and was hungry to learn more.

"So, what is going on with you? Casanova mentioned I should ask you about your well-being and state of mind. What is going on?"

"What is not going on, Wren? Anyway, I do not want to bother you about that now. You just woke up this morning. You need time to relax your mind."

"Girl, my mind and body are too relaxed. I am so anxious to leave this place and get into my word. I am going to research the bible and any other helpful resources. Casanova and I had a chance to talk after the doctors left me alone. The Lord has been changing him; he appears different. I will be honest, though. I know we can remain great friends, but I am unsure if I am the Lord's wife for him."

"Wait, so are you thinking of divorcing him? You cannot do that, sis; you have no grounds! I retract because you must live in peace, though."

"I did not say all of that, Cartel. I am just taking it one day at a time. He put me through things that require healing and forgiveness that only the Lord can help me do."

"He has been seeking the Lord and getting some counseling. He loves you for real, sis! However, I know his words and other levels of abuse were too much. I am just sorry that I did not help you. I did not know what to believe. Casanova did come clean about it to George and me. Speaking of George, I cannot say that he and I will make it. I asked him to file for a divorce, but he has not done it yet."

"So, why would you ask your husband for a divorce? You have no grounds. Wait, did he cheat or something?" Wren asked, grabbing her friend's hand from the bed's side rail.

"That is the only way out. Yes, he cheated with a one-night stand who got lucky. She is carrying my husband's seed."

Wren thought for a moment to herself. She looked over at Cartel. "Cartel. I do not believe this story. He might have cheated, but something does not sound right here. I know women can get pregnant, and all it takes is once, but something is not clear here."

"Like, what do you mean?" Cartel asked, pulling her hand away from Wren.

"Have we seen this chick? Has she been in the shop? Lonely or miserable women will prey on others' happiness, especially a great marriage. She could have been pregnant. Have you talked to your husband to find out when this happened? Have you counted the days/months to see if this could be his child? I do not trust it. She was waiting on the sidelines for an opportunity to find a weakness in your marriage. She could have known about your struggles with staying pregnant. Do not give up on your husband that fast. At least talk to him and get some answers."

Cartel thought Wren had taken Casanova's side for a moment, but then the words she spoke made sense. "Look at God! He used my friend to counsel me. I received it well. No, I have not allowed him an opportunity to provide me with details. I could not listen to it, Wren! And something in my spirit tells me there is more to the story, but I could not dare find out more. I was too afraid and had no support. You were here fighting for your life; I had no one."

"I am sure you had your husband and, most importantly, God. You knew God would bring me out, so you should not have been worrying. God knew I needed rest, some peace."

"Wow, which is the same thing your mother said." Cartel explained.

"My mother, she was here?" Wren asked. Curious as to why.

"Yes, ma'am. She got to the hospital as soon as she received word. She was a prayer warrior too. She kept us all in line, and we needed her. You need her too."

"I could not agree more. The sound of you saying my mother was here gave me a feeling of joy. I will tell my brother Steven to bring her up here to see me."

"What? Oh yes, God touched you for real while you were resting. I am so glad you are allowing Sharon a second chance. I wish I could do the same for Susan."

"Susan, who is that? The only Susan we know together is the flower shop owner."

"Yes, that one. Susan told your mother, Sharon, that she is my birth mother. So, George followed up with her and confirmed the same news. Last, George set up delivery of roses to the shop, and sure enough, she hand-delivered them to me. She wanted to spill out the details, and it blew me away. I instantly hated her!"

"Hate is such a strong word. You do not hate her; you are just upset with her. So, is she your mother?"

"I do not know. I do not care at the moment. I am an adult, and I have too much on my plate to deal with her."

"The things you used to say to me at one point. Let us explore that - *If only you had a chance to see your mother again.* And I know this woman is not Trina, the mother you know, but it might be beneficial to see if there is any truth to her story."

"In time, my friend, but my marriage comes first. I need to chat with my man so we can find out the truth about this baby."

"I know that's right." Wren held up her hand to the high-five Cartel. "So, what else is new? How is Garcia?"

"Girl, I will let her tell you what she's been digging up." Cartel laughed aloud.

One week later

Sounds of police and ambulance sirens filled the neighborhood near Jamie's house. Streaks of blood trailed from the house's front door to the sidewalk. Jamie sat on the ground in tears holding her right arm. Two police officers spoke to her as the ambulance crew rushed to assist her. She struggled to explain her story. Jamie's allusion was filled with emotions and confusion. What just occurred was unexpected. She grabbed a tissue from one of the officers to clear her face.

Wren and Cartel pulled up to the scene in total disbelief realizing their friend's story was factual. Both women prayed along the way, hoping it was not valid. Jamie was such a kind-hearted, sweet person who would betray her in such a way? Jamie refused a trip to the hospital. The paramedics urged her to go as blood gushed from her arm. The pressure was not enough, and the fear of losing too much blood was their concern.

Jamie's husband got questioned about his actions during the attack. Police were talking with him, gathering a statement for an arrest. Her nephew, Jordan, could get heard crying exoterically as his mother, Kimmel, got hauled off to the backseat of a squad car. A police officer hugged him tightly, reassuring him his mother would be fine.

"Jamie! You need to go to the hospital." Wren encouraged her to do so after the police allowed her to come near.

"After all that I have done for Kimmel. This is what she does to her son and me? She smiled in my face for years. Who knows how long she had been sleeping with my husband? I worked late, overnight shifts at the hospital, trying to provide for my siblings all those nights. While she slept with my husband," Jamie yelled out. "Just let me kill her now!"

Cartel remained a few steps away in prayer. Cartel had no idea what to say or do to help Jamie. Her heart wept for her. Although she could understand her pain regarding a cheating spouse, she could never imagine it being a sibling or family member. *Lord, we need your help, and we need it now.* She whispered.

Jamie temporarily lost consciousness; her eyes rolled as she slowly returned. "Ma'am, we are taking you to the hospital now." One of the paramedics informed. Jamie no longer resisted. Their precautions were valid; they helped her onto the stretcher and lifted her into the back of the van.

"Can I come with her?" Wren asked one of the paramedics.

"Sure, you can sit right here beside her."

Wren hoped in and waved to Cartel, who agreed to meet at the hospital. As they left the scene, Jamie reached for Wren's hand. Wren pulled in close to her as she knew her friend needed whatever support she could provide.

"Wren, Jordan…my nephew. How could she do this to him?"

"What did she do to Jordan? How did this start anyway? But, if it is too much to say, just rest. We need to ensure that baby is fine and that arm gets the treatment."

"She stabbed me. I cannot believe she swung that knife at me. She could have killed my unborn child and me."

"But she did not, and you are alive and well. Do not think about what could have happened. Praise God for what did not happen."

Jamie nodded, agreeing, "Wait, did you just mention God?"

"I did. And I know I have not had a chance to chat since I left the hospital. And we have so much to catch up on. I want you to stay calm and let these medical professionals help you. Ok?"

"Yes, but I am so angry, Wren! Did you hear Jordan crying so loudly? Then my husband, the look on his face. I bet he knew all the time." Jamie's face saddened.

Wren sat unsure of what Jamie was referring to regarding Karl knowing. She did not want to press for more than Jamie wanted to share. She knew Jamie and Kimmel had a fistfight leading to a knife being brandished and used. The rest of the story was still unclear. Wren grabbed a tissue to wipe the tears forming in Jamie's eyes.

"Wren, she slept with my husband! She said that Jordan's father is Karl. Can you believe this mess? I want to hurt both so badly right now. When she yelled out the news, his face, right before slicing me with that knife, his expression told it all."

"Now wait a minute, sis! How could this go unnoticed for so many years? How do you know she is telling the truth?"

"Again, by the guilty look on that bastard's face. He was guilty as charged."

Wren lowered her head. Not one encouraging word came to mind. The news was devasting. And not only that but her friend got assaulted. She held her hand and remained silent the remainder of the ride to the hospital.

Later that evening, Jamie got released from the emergency department with instructions on treating her wound. The baby was in decent shape, and her pregnancy was not at risk for premature labor. She was close to five months, so knowing the baby was fine was good. Jamie's mother, Cena Brownstone, met at Jamie's house along with Cartel and Wren.

Jamie's home looked like a crime scene. Kimmel and her fight started in the kitchen and ended in the living room. Jamie sat up a broken lamp. The shade frame was bent out of shape and ruined. Wren and Cartel began picking up pieces of a broken vase.

"Jamie, I cannot believe that you and Kimmel would fistfight," Cena, their mother, said as she glanced around the living room in total shock.

"Mom, this is what I attempted to explain to you the other week. I felt in my spirit something was coming. I never knew that something involved my husband, though."

"Well, I will not say Kimmel was the only one wrong here. Your husband is accountable as well. Your sister is a beautiful petite dark, brown-skinned girl. He could have been waiting for her to become an adult."

"Are your serious right now, mother!?" Jamie asked, taking a seat down on her couch. "Who cares how beautiful Kimmel is? Some things are just off-limits."

"Yes, I am serious. Your husband should have acted like an adult man and not lusted after a child. You know I speak facts, so do not get all in your feelings." She added, fixing pillows on the couch.

"You know, I could easily be very disrespectful right now. Maybe if you were not out in the streets experimenting with every drug on the planet and men, your daughter could have been home with you."

"Now, Jamie!" Cartel called her name. "At the end of the day, Cena is still your mother."

"She never acted like a mother. That is why I had to raise my siblings in the first place. All she cared about were men and drugs. I was the one who had to raise them, attend, and pay for college myself and put them through school. All my siblings had was me. I am their parental figure." Jamie's voice sharpened, looking at her mother.

Cena walked up to Jamie. "Is that all you think of me?" she asked, whisking a slap across her face. "Don't you ever talk to me that way!"

"Get out of my house, lady!" Jamie yelled, fighting hard not to swing back at her mother.

"I will gladly leave. Furthermore, I do not care what I have done. Those are your siblings. I was not well. It was your responsibility as the oldest child to step up. Do not act like you are a great saint because you raised your siblings. Also, Kimmel has been putting up with your high-yellow arrogant self for years. Now I understand. I will be back for my twins. I do not want them in your custody another day."

"That is funny. The twins are sixteen years old, and now you want to be a mother. Laughable!" Jamie followed her mother to the front door. "If the twins want to stay with me, you will not force them to leave with you."

"I said, what I said, Jamie! I will return for my twins when they leave school today. I can only imagine how they low-key feel about you as well." Cena responded, leaving the house.

"I am so sorry all of this is happening, Jamie," Wren said, embracing her in a hug.

"Hey, these are not new actions from my mother. She never had anything nice or encouraging to say to me anyway." Jamie removed herself from Wren's arm. "I need to take a seat; she sat back on the couch.

"You rest while Cartel and I clean up," Wren told her.

"You know, your mom appears jealous of you." Cartel spoke up.

"Yeah, I figured that out years ago. Remember when she came to Karl and my wedding? Instead of congratulating me, she showed up to say how she disliked me. She told me I was arrogant that day as well. She is the reason Kimmel developed those thoughts of me. Regardless, I never thought Kimmel would cross me the way she did. My sister had a child with my husband. My nephew is also my stepson! How do you explain that to a child?"

" When he's old enough to receive it. I remember how bogus your mom acted at your wedding, but she apologized many times over the years. She blamed the drugs for those actions, remember?" Wren recalled.

"Yes, I remember, so I continued to allow her to come around."

"People tend to blame the drugs or alcohol for altering their behavior, but the thoughts are authentic," Cartel began, "I gather your mom is jealous of your strength. You raised your siblings, graduated from college, and have a career and a husband. Enough said."

"Whelp, I am not sure if that is accurate, but she made it clear that she does not like me on several occasions. I only put up with her this long because of the twins. I allow her to come by and visit them and Kimmel. Plus, I could tell my mother loves her grandson, Jordan. He gave her the desire to stay clean."

"Do you want me to call the county jail to check on your husband?" Wren asked.

"No, he is not in jail. He went over to his mother's house to clear his head. He was texting while we were at the hospital. He was making sure the baby and I was doing well. I told him we were fine, and then I blocked his number. I do not want to speak to him either."

"What are you going to do then? Just sit in this house alone. Your mother is coming back for the twins. Your sister is in jail. Where did they take Jordan? Did Karl tell you that in the message?"

"Karl has Jordan with him. Go figure!"

"Well, I am not going to add to your frustration, but you need to talk to your husband about Jordan being his son." Wren encouraged.

"There is nothing to discuss. Jordan is his son. People teased Karl and me about Jordan for many years, stating he looked like he could be our child. Remember that?" Jamie recollected.

"Yeah, but we all blew that off. You and Kimmel favor so much that Jordan could pass off as your son."

"For the sake of Jordan, who I love so much. I am going to seek the truth. He deserves to know if Karl is his father. I will ask Karl to get a DNA test done. If he wants to save our marriage, he better move forward with it." Jamie told them.

"Wow, girl! You are strong! Here you stand, pregnant, attacked, and cheated on, and still, you find it in your heart to do the right thing." Wren pointed out.

"Yeah, well, Jordan is innocent. The love should not change in any way towards him. I would need to take it one day at a time. Try to keep the peace until I deliver my baby, then decide what is best for me next." Jamie explained.

"Honestly, we all have some soul searching to do. Wren, you are still contemplating leaving Casanova. And I understand you want to continue in your peace, but you have to think about this from a biblical perspective. You can either believe God to continue to

lead him or take matters in your hands and leave."
Cartel advised, taking a seat on the couch next to Jamie.

"Yes, that's true." Wren agreed.

"Then, I must figure out my mess with George.
Jamie, he got some random female pregnant. That is the
news I received when I left the shop that day. I could
not confide in you and Garcia at dinner that evening. I
needed time to let it all soak in."

"Oh wow! I would have never guessed," Jamie
frowned at her. "You two have an authentic
relationship. I would have never thought he would go
there. Does he doubt that you will carry a baby to full
term?"

"Yep, and then to add to it. Susan from the
flower shop thinks she is my birth mother. You might
have heard that part when we were at the hospital with
Wren."

"Wait, I am still trying to digest the cheating
spouse. That is too much! I heard Sharon mentioned
Susan to you; I closed it off. How? Your parents are
deceased. I am so confused." Jamie said, scratching her
head.

"Yes, I am too, but this reminds me that everyone is going through something. God never promised us that this life would be easy. Every day we are dealing with our flesh and other people's demons. We must look for the best in each situation and decision we make." Cartel added.

"That is true, Cartel. We all should go home to think, pray, and ask God to help us with our situations. I will stand by whatever decisions either of you women makes." Wren supported.

"I second that! We are not in the best mental state to make decisions at this time," Jamie agreed. "Well, I know I am not in the best mental state. I want to kill my sister, and if I see her, I will kill her."

"You will not kill your sister, Jamie. Do not even begin to let those thoughts fester. It will become a reality. Remember, it starts in our thoughts. Rebuke it now!" Cartel explained.

"You are right, I guess. But in all seriousness, Wren. I am not sure why you are considering leaving Casanova but think about it a little more. That man has become some teacher or life coach. I saw him at the grocery store a while back. He went into the word and how he believed God for your awakening. He encouraged me to get into that word." Jamie told them.

"Jamie, I have told Cartel and you about his abuse before. The day I had the accident, he said words that cut like a knife. The disrespect was so deep that I got lost in it. I ran off the road and hit a huge tree without thinking."

"Wow! I did not know an argument with him caused the accident. I am so sorry all this abuse went unnoticed. And yes, I heard you, but I should have done more," Jamie apologized. "Hey, Cartel, is that grounds for divorce?"

"It is abuse, and those are my grounds," Wren responded before Cartel could. "If your husband does not have anything nice to say to you. All you hear is what you are not to him. It can eventually make a negative impact on your life."

"That is true, " Jamie agreed.

"With that, you get some rest, Jamie. We will all check back with each other in due season." Cartel reiterated, getting up to leave Jamie's house.

Jamie walked both ladies to the front door. They grabbed hands, prayed, and gave each other hugs believing God heard their prayers and would lead them from this point.

In Casanova's hands was certified divorce paperwork the county sheriff delivered. He stood in his home shared with his parents, watching the sheriff drive off. In disbelief, he thought Wren and him had been making noteworthy progress rebuilding their marriage. They had been on several dates over the past weeks and talking daily. And although Casanova had not moved back into Wren's home, he did not think it would lead to a permanent separation.

His mother, Anna, stood behind him with a saddened facial expression. She was still not a fan of Wren but seeing her son heartbroken was not a win for her. She struggled to find the right words to say. Careful with word choice as Casanova knew her true thoughts of Wren.

His father, Gregory, also stood behind him in disbelief. Gregory was not a fan of divorce and wanted his son's marriage to survive. For the last few weeks, he had been praying and believing with his son that God would heal the pain in Wren's heart and their marriage. Gregory had no words. Regardless of how many encouraging words he could say, nothing would help the pain his son was experiencing now.

Casanova looked down at the paperwork. His first thought was to call Wren and ask her why, but he realized that would not change anything. He turned to face his parents holding the paperwork up in the air. "Well, you win, mother! Go ahead and tell me; you told me so!" he said.

"I would not do that, Casanova. I know you loved that girl. Just make sure you contact the Trading law firm, you did not have a prenuptial agreement, and that girl will aim for all your money."

"Really, Anna? Just be silent if you do not have anything encouraging to say now." Gregory demanded.

"I agree with that, dad. I need some time alone anyway. I will be back in a few hours." Casanova told them.

"Casanova, do not call that woman. Give her time!" Anna suggested.

"Casanova, just because she filed does not mean she will go through with it. You two had some severe storms early in the marriage. Have you sat down and examined yourself? What makes you strike this woman every time she disagrees with you? What makes you say degrading words to her? Can you sustain in a union with a strong, educated woman?" Gregory asked.

"Educated?" Anna whispered under her breath.

"Dad, I have not hit this woman or said anything degrading to her since she has been home from the hospital. We have been nothing but friends, enjoying each other's company. That is why this paperwork makes no sense to me. I am going to her house to speak with her about it."

"Oh Boy, don't beg anyone to stay with you," Anna told him, shaking her head.

"One more word, Anna!" Gregory warned, pointing his finger at her.

"As I told him before, he can do better! But in all honestly, I think I should be the one to talk to Wren. She needs a mother figure. I think that I can get through to her."

"She has a mother and a good one at that. I had a chance to get to know her mother while Wren was in a coma. The woman is everything amazing! And no, I do not want you speaking to my wife about anything. If I have any chance, you would be sure to ruin it."

"Her mother is a probationer, Casanova. There is no good in that!" Anna reminded him.

Responding to Anna would be a continuous uphill battle. Instead, Casanova side-chatted with his father and then parted ways. His mind was on reconciling with his wife, Wren. He needed her to understand that he was in it for the long haul. Giving up was not an option for him, no matter what.

Later that evening, Cartel met with her cousin Liza at Liza's house. After ignoring Susan's conversation for a while, it was time for her to learn the truth. Liza prepared dinner. She placed their plates on the table. After grace, they began to eat their meals.

Between bites, Cartel attempted to start the conversation. She did not want to learn that Trina was not her birth mother. That would also mean Liza would not be her first cousin either. She placed down her fork to brace herself. "Ok, cousin. I need to ask you something."

"Wait, let me help you. No, I did not meet up with the Black man from the park anymore." Liza settled.

"Um, could you not refer to him as the Black man from the park? His name was Henry Stalling. Let us not forget you spent several months talking on the phone to this man. I could have sworn you mentioned falling in love for a second." Cartel teased her.

"Ok, don't be ridiculous," Liza responded, moving her plate away. Her appetite now ruined. "Now, what's up?"

"Be honest, did your aunt Trina have any natural children?"

"Um, yes, I am looking at her. My bi-racial cousin." Liza pestered.

"I said, natural children. She adopted me."

"Who told you that? " Liza asked, now puzzled.

"What do you know, Liza, because I know you heard something throughout life?"

Liza took a moment to collect her thoughts. "Listen, Cartel. All jokes aside, ok? I am not sure who your birth mother is, but I know. I do know that…that…my aunt Trina…did…I mean…did not…have any natural children." It pained Liza to deliver that news. She and Cartel had grown so close over the years that she hoped nothing would change.

Cartel sat back in her chair. She hoped to hear Liza confirm that she was Trina's natural daughter. A range of emotions fluttered her. Sad that Trina was not her mother, upset that Susan could be her mother, betrayed by Liza for withholding such information, yet mad that she had such a bogus childhood. At the same time, she was pissed that her birth mother watched from afar. She reminded herself that she was a child of God and could get through anything with that. "Thank you, Liza, for the information." Cartel lowered her head to the table.

"How did this even come about? Why are you questioning Aunt Trina?"

Cartel lifted her head to speak to her. "You know, I found out from Susan a month ago. Susan, the floral shop client of mine. Susan mentioned she is my birth mother. I still cannot process it. I guess I do not want to believe the reality."

"And what proof did she have? I know Aunt Trina did not have children, but that Susan lady still would need to prove she is your birth mother."

"She did. She told me the story about how she and my father met. She was being a hot mama and got pregnant by a Black man. She got scared, hid the pregnancy, then gave my dad total custody of me. She knew too much, Liza. She knew about my mom, Trina, adopting me, and she even had the original birth record wrinkled up in her purse. I do not want her to be my mother for some reason."

"I know, cousin. And I know I make so many jokes about Black people mainly because our family raised us to dislike Black people. Why? I have no idea. I have heard so many reasons, but the truth is none of the grounds make any sense. My mother, Angela, could never understand why her sister, Trina, would marry a drug-dealing Black man when their parents worked so hard to have a great life. Then, she got killed during a drug deal? That never sat right with the family. But for some reason, they tried hard to accept you, though."

"Yeah, but I could feel the difference. I did not feel connected to anyone. Something did not feel right. Around my dad's family, I felt like I belonged. Yet around my mom's family, something felt strange. Even with you and me. I knew we were good friends, but the family bond part was not there."

"Seriously? I thought we were tight. I mean, you were the only Black woman I hung around." Liza replied, trying to joke and lighten the load.

"Yeah, but the rest of our cousins, well, your cousins did not put forth any effort to get to know me. I used to think it was because I got separated when I entered the system, but now it all makes sense."

"Well, do not be sad about it. You have made a great life for yourself. You have a great husband who loves you more than anything. I care a lot about you as well. I can see why Susan wanted you to know this information."

"Thanks, Dr. Liza Littlejohn!" Cartel teased.

"And Cartel, I do miss Henry Stallings so much!" Liza admitted, throwing her hands up in the air. "Truth is, I do not want to like him because he is Black, and our family will never approve of him. Yet, I miss him, and I cannot help it. I do like him; I love him!"

"I knew it. You took after your aunt Trina. You are attracted to chocolate brothas!"

"No, I just fell for that Black man. He is so intelligent to me. Our conversations were so deep. His outlook on life was at another level. Regardless of the conversation topic, we agreed on everything. We just matched perfectly."

"Why haven't you called him, Liza?"

"Because he is a Black man, Cartel! We just discussed how our family dislikes Black people. Your dad, uncle Jesse, had the hardest time gaining acceptance into this family."

"Yeah, but that did not stop my mom, Trina, from marrying him. She did not allow others to ruin her opportunity at true love. You should take note of that."

"Yeah, true, " Liza got up to clear the table. "Do you want some dessert?"

"Nope, I am good. I am going to head home. I need to have a conversation with my husband. We hit a tough spot in our marriage recently. I am sitting here talking to you and thinking about my mom Trina. The fight she endured for my dad. Going against the grain and marrying my dad. All I ever heard was how genuine of a relationship they had. They were real friends. It made me realize, just now, that I have a real friend at home too. It is time for me to face the issue and figure out what is next for us."

"Well, that sounds better than chocolate cake anyway. Heck, I might just call up Mr. Henry tonight too." Liza responded. "Well, I enjoyed your company, cousin. And just know blood couldn't make us any closer."

"I agree, Liza. Thank you for letting me know the truth about my mother, Trina. Knowing that she loved me enough to make me her own is everything. I will never allow Susan or anyone to take her mother's title. And I agree that you should call Henry this evening because true love asks for nothing."

"That is so true, and I am going to call him. I hope he missed me as much as I have missed him. And as for you, do not stop being my friend. Better yet, do not stop being my cousin."

"Of course, nothing changes. I agreed with your statement that blood could not make us closer. Enjoy your night!" Cartel retorted, leaving Liza's home.

Cartel returned to a bed of roses spread from the front door leading up the stairs to their master bedroom suite. Candle-light dinner was set up in their bedroom. Cartel thought the setup was strange as their home had plenty of room to eat downstairs. She glanced around for George, who stood behind her. She jumped as they met eyes. She smiled at him. "What are you trying to accomplish with food in the bedroom?" She asked.

"I was not sure if you had eaten yet or were tired and ready for bed. I just made it convenient for you either way."

Cartel giggled at the thought of George's response. He said the silliest things at times. "I am not hungry. I had a long day. I finally spoke to Liza about my mother, Trina. And sure enough, Trina was not my birth mother."

"And how does that make you feel, better or worse?" George asked, not shocked by the news.

"I don't know what I feel right now, George. Honestly, I want to put away the birth mother drama. It is time that we decide on ourselves."

George took her hand, leading her to sit beside him on the bed. He removed her shoes to relax her a bit. "You know, the decision is yours. I meant what I said from the beginning. I am not leaving you. There is only one woman for me, and that is you. No matter how much you dislike me right now, I am willing to wait for it."

"I am tired of fighting with you about this woman. I know she had the baby. I know you have visited her. What do you think? Just lay it on me. I can take it."

"I will tell you what I think as soon as you answer me about the decision. It is yours, and I have been waiting on this for a while. If the baby boy is mine, are you leaving me, or are we going to work through it?"

Cartel took a deep breath, pausing before she spoke to it. She had prayed to God for strength to help her deal with the unknown. "You know what, I know what I have. I know what we have, and I refuse to let another woman destroy what we have built."

"Do you think you're the wife God had for me?" George asked.

"What do you think?" Cartel responded with a question.

"When I heard you speak to Casanova about marrying Wren without allowing the Lord to lead, I started to think about us. I asked you to marry me without consulting the Lord. And you said yes. Did God give you something in your heart that confirmed I was the mate for you?"

"Nope, because I was unlearned at that point. I answered without hesitation when you asked because it just felt right."

"I thought so. And I agree. It just felt right. So, I begin to pray and ask for forgiveness regarding marrying you too soon or marrying you if it was not God's will. I prayed about honoring vows as the bible speaks to honor our word—the promises we make before the Lord. There is no; I made a mistake. With that, I asked the Lord to help us. Help us to learn from each other and how to please each other. Help us to grow and only have eyes for each other…even if we cannot birth our children."

"What do you mean, you have a son now? I am the one who cannot bear children."

"Her son's name is Benjamin. Benjamin, junior. When I went to her home to meet him, I met Benjamin, the senior, at the door. All three of us had a real conversation. The same night she was at the club, she was sulking. Benjamin, the senior, and she just had a major break-up. They were together for two years. From what I understood, Benjamin, Sr, cheated on her, which was the cause of the breakup."

"Really?" Cartel questioned.

"Yes, and simultaneously, you and I just lost another baby. It was a perfect night for revenge/rebound sex for her. I met up with her during a season of pain. As it turns out, I never had sex with that woman. I went to her home, but I never had sex with her. Thank you, God! Cartel, I cannot praise God enough. That woman told me I was drunk as a skunk, but I could not get with her that way. Regardless of how hard she tried to get me to go there. I fell asleep the next morning still in my clothes."

"So, how do you know if that story is factual? How do you know she is not just saying that to get her man, Benjamin, the senior, back? He was right there as she told the story, correct?"

"Yes, he was. But Cartel, I could not remember that night for anything. Her story was so unclear. Before I got saved, I had been drunk before. Even during those times, I knew my actions. Something was not clear with her story. Furthermore, she was already pregnant by Benjamin, and that baby had the largest set of nostrils on him. He shares that feature with his large-nose father," George laughed. "It is their family trait. The boy is his, and I never cheated on my wife."

"So, why did you want me to spill out my decision first?"

"It was a test of your love for me. If you chose to walk, I had no choice but to understand. I kept telling you something was wrong with that woman's story, but I had nothing to stand on. She wants to apologize to you formally, but I told her we are good. It is not necessary now."

"Oh no, it is necessary, and I will pay her and baby Benjamin a visit soon. She took a shot at my marriage and almost destroyed it."

"Understood. But God!" George exclaimed.

"So, this happened the night I lost the baby at the hospital? They kept me overnight for observation because of the chest pain and irregular heartbeats, and you went out and almost cheated on me."

"Yes, it was that night, Cartel. I went home to get items to return to the hospital, and I never did. I told you I had fallen asleep."

"Wow! The truth does come out in the light at some point. Regardless, Susan told me to be careful of these women. A mother knows."

"A mother knows. Did you just refer to Susan as your mother?" George questioned.

"A wise man will hear and increase his learning, and a man of understanding shall attain into wise counsel. Susan shared words of wisdom with me the night she confessed to being my mother. She also counseled. She advised about women who prey on a great marriage. That woman had been to our shop several times, getting her hair colored by Valerie. She knew I was having trouble carrying a child. She knew who you were in the club and took a shot during a weak time in our life. The devil knows when and where to aim," Cartel shook her head. "No matter how much I disliked Susan that day, her counsel struck me like a lightning bolt. It made me think for a moment, but the trust got broken between you and me. So it eventually left me."

"Understood. Proverbs is full of scriptures that speak to emotions. It speaks to the power of the tongue as well. It is a book of wise counsel; wisdom—King Solomon; insight over foolishness. I was very foolish to walk in the hands of that Jezebel-spirited woman. My stupidity and distrust in God led me right into the hands of the enemy. Taking matters into my hands almost cost my marriage, wife, and best friend."

"You got that right." Cartel agreed.

" Yet going back to the father to admit my wrongdoings and pleading for forgiveness and a second chance placed pressure on that woman's heart to no longer live with the lie. She called Benjamin and me over at the same time. I do not know if she needed one of us to protect her from the other as we received the news, but I am glad it is his child and not mine. The baby boy's name is going to get changed to Benjamin junior. Benjamin senior looked at the baby and did not attempt to deny him. All he said was, change his name to junior."

"I am glad the baby is not yours either. I am still asking God for a baby or two of our own," She hugged George and kissed him on the cheek. "And now, I am hungry. I am ready to eat what you have on that table!" Cartel smiled, relieved her husband's actions did not include cheating on her. She realized the trust needed restoration and that George was a man, human. He must fight against the flesh daily, just as she. Regardless, she knew he was good for her and vice versa. And with that, she was content with working through whatever it took to rebuild their union.

"We got steak and potato. We got red wine and chocolate cake. The cake is from the one and only; I had to make that stop. Best chocolate cake ever!" George took her hand and led her to the table. He gave all praises to God for opening the door of restoration. To him, all praises, glory, and honor!

Chapter Five: Restoration Time

Liza met up with Henry Stallings at one of Chicago's most talked-about soul food restaurants. The lines were out the door, and the reservation list just closed after adding their name. They sat in her car, deciding if they should stay or leave. Henry, not interested in eating food, was more concerned about why Liza wanted a second chance.

"While we wait, may I understand what's behind the meeting request?" he asked.

"Of course, Henry, I tried to explain to you on the phone the other night. I was wrong for not allowing us to move forward. I was raised to stay away from Black people. Most of you do not want anything in life but crime and bad health."

He laughed. "Is that what white people think of us? I find that interesting because this so-called America got built off our backs. Nothing is given to my people. In contrast, others receive a wealth of inheritance passed down through generations from our ancestors' recipes, hours of labor, and other business ideas. We invented much more than you realize. For example, half of these well-known commercial chicken fast food joints are the recipe of an unknown Black person. White folks cannot cook; we all know that."

"That is not true, Henry. We can cook!" Liza defended.

"My point is, Liza, just as you drew offense to my white folks cannot cook stereotype, I drew offense to your comment about all Black people want is a life of crime and bad health. The truth is, we have ghetto Black people. The truth is, we have intelligent Black people who work hard for a well-deserved honest living. Yet every news outlet targets our communities and inflates our characters into the narrative you describe. Those news reporters who zoom in on the misguided Black people do not speak for half of my intelligent, hard-working people. Like every race, Whites, Mexicans, Puerto Ricans, and Chinese folks, you have some ghetto ones and some who are hardworking, honest living folks. One day, you must decide to get to know a person for who they are and not the color of their skin."

"See, this is what I explained to my cousin, Cartel. You do not speak like the average Black man. You are so wise, so intelligent." Liza complimented.

"No, there are many intelligent brothas out there. Again, you are adhering to stereotypes. So, why did you call me again? You do realize that I am Black as they come." He laughed, looking at his arms.

"I do realize your skin is brown, Henry. And honestly, I tried to forget about you. Why? Because I knew my family would hate the thought of it. A successful white primary care provider in love with a Black man."

"You mean a successful Black man who invested well in life, made good on his investments, and owns profitable businesses."

"Does that equate to street talk, like selling drugs? You told me this before but never quite detailed the types of businesses or investments."

"Is that a need to know when you are just dating someone? I would think the main goal is to identify the Spirit. Who is this person? Is this person a good fit in character for me? Then, of course, yes, later, you learn more as those decisions get made."

"Well, I am in love with you. So, when do I learn more about how you provide and make a living?"

"Liza, please do not get offended by what I must say. Just because you fall for me does not mean I have fallen for you. Do not get emotionally involved so fast. I move at distinct levels. If you find a man moving fast, he is hiding something. I think you are a great woman, but your arrogancy and privileged comments annoy me."

"Now that was rude, Henry. I am not arrogant or feel privileged, and now you are stereotyping me. Privileged is what they say about the average white person."

"No, I am telling you my thoughts of you as an individual. I like you, but I am not in love with you. We have had some of the best conversations over the last few months. I can see this potentially growing into something long-term, but we will take our time. You think you are royalty!" Henry laughed again.

Liza glanced at the clock on her dashboard. Quoted a twenty-minute wait, she knew it would not be good if they missed her name call. She made eye contact with Henry, who was busy clicking on his cell phone. She ignored his comment about her being royalty. He had her mistaken as one of those white people who received an inheritance or some generous sum of money to purchase a home or business development. No, she was from an average living white family who stressed the importance of a college education as a pillar to the kick-off of an admired career. However, his reluctance to allow himself to love her was aggravating. She knew he felt it. He just did not want to admit it.

"Are you ok over there?" he looked up from his phone, and their eyes met.

"Yes, I am about to go check the list. We are getting closer to my name being called," she responded. She reached for the door.

He grabbed her hand. "I can check this list; you stay inside and keep warm. I got this beautiful!" He smiled, exiting the vehicle. Henry felt their levels of society were not aligned, but he liked her and was eager to explore her anyway.

Liza texted Cartel, *"I made a mistake about Henry. I do not think he is into me anymore. I might have disappointed him when I left him in the park that evening. The conversations have changed."* Cartel responded, *"If he was into you before, he still is into you now. I forgave my husband, and your text message is killing my evening, later cousin. Love you!"*

Henry returned to the car. She asked, "Did I hurt you when I walked away from you in the park? If I did, I am sorry. Your demeanor is different now. I must have hurt you in some way."

Henry released a burst of gut-wrenching laughter. He nodded his head, unable to stop laughing. "Girl, now that was good! Some white people stuff, but I get it. You want to know how I truly feel about you. Correct?" He shrugged his shoulders, then turned to face her.

"Yes, because we haven't spoken in a long time, and I want to know if I still have a chance or am wasting my time."

"Ok, all jokes to the side. I felt crushed for about a week after you walked off and stopped calling me. You also ignored my calls. I thought we had something special, but then I thought that if someone could just walk away so simply, nothing was ever there. I got raised to believe if you have something good, you fight for it. I mean, fighting your way to a criminal case is not the answer but fighting for the union. I was willing to fight for the woman who stood before me. I was willing to do whatever it took to sustain what I thought was special. So, now the ball is in your court. I am not fighting for someone who could walk away from me at the dime drop."

"I saw your calls but did not know how to proceed."

"Do you know how to proceed now? If so, enlighten me."

"For us, to protect what we have, I must go against my family. They dislike Black people. My aunt, Cartel's mother, Trina. She married a Black man and almost got disowned by our family. She held her grounds, and I must do the same for us no matter how my family feels."

"Well, you let me know how that works out for you. After that conversation with your racist family, let me know if you are still for us. We will decide what is next for us after. I think that woman just called your name. Let us go inside."

"Yeah, she did. And, Henry, I meant what I said. I want this to work. Not speaking to you drove me nuts. But I got this now, and I am not going anywhere!" Liza opened her car door. She looked back at him. "Now, let's go eat."

Jamie fell asleep on her living room couch. Her husband, Karl, came home to address the issue surrounding his potential son, Jordan. Although she had him blocked on her cellular device, the locks to the door remained unchanged.

"Jamie!" Karl called out her name, trying not to startle her.

She looked up at him, happy to see him. "Hey! You finally came home!"

He sat down next to her on the couch. "Jamie, I need to talk to you. I had time to think and figure out what is best for us."

She sat up to face him. Her smile faded as she braced herself for the words that would follow. She grabbed his face, making sure he looked her in the eyes. "Tell me, what's on your mind."

"I am going to move in with my mother for a while. Jordan is confused about everything that has transpired, including knowing I am his father. He asks about you often; he misses you. I know you miss him too, but I am unsure how this will work. You will never forgive me enough to get past it. And I cannot allow you to change towards him or mistreat him."

"Mistreat him? Um, that is my nephew. I love him just as much as you do. Let us not get silly here. And what about the child I am carrying? We prayed so long for this bundle of joy. And now, the baby will enter a divided family?"

"I think you should give me full custody of our baby. I will raise both children without all the stress from your sister and you."

"I am not one of those mothers who give their child up. I know people must make the best decisions for themselves, and I would never disrespect anyone who has made that decision. As for this baby, I ask God for this baby, just as you did. And I will never give my baby up!"

"I knew this would not be easy with you. I spoke to Kimmel about it. She agreed it would be best if I raised our son alone and not with you."

"Of course, she would. Karl! She does not want to see you with me. Do you not understand that part?"

Jamie stood up and walked away from him. He sounded nuts! *How could he not see this coming?*

Karl followed her into the kitchen. He was not there to hurt his wife, but his love for his son and unborn child was greater. He was willing to take that chance if he had to lose his wife over it. "Jamie, listen."

"Karl, let me ask you something, and please be honest. Do you love my sister?" she interrupted him.

"Yes, as my son's mother, I loved joking with your sister. She saw me as a man. You wanted me to be honest; there it is."

"So, you like her a lot. I get it. Do you still love me? Wait, are you still in love with me?"

"I do love you. And no, I do not think I am in love with you anymore. Jamie, we never had any time for ourselves. When I met you, you were in college and raising your siblings. We never had time to date. We rarely had time to enjoy each other. I was brought into this family and adapted to all of you simultaneously. I got caught up in your looks and your strength. You are amazing as a person and a great friend, but I am not sure if we are great together. And now, we were only supposed to be great friends. You were not supposed to be my wife."

The sting from the words that rolled from his tongue. Tears immediately streamed from Jamie's eyes. Her heart shattered at the thought of a broken marriage. Divorce would have never been an option for her. The man who stood before her was unknown. He never spoke to her in this way. She wondered what had gotten into him. "The devil is a lie!' she quoted. It was not the time to cry; it was the time to fight.

"The devil?" Karl repeated. "I don't know, Jamie, maybe I am saying things I do not mean," he admitted, pulling her close in his arms. "I do not know how to fix this. I messed up so badly with you."

She wiped her tears away. "You can start by telling me where I went wrong as a wife. How did I miss so much of the time you needed or time you had to spend with my sister?"

Karl walked her back to the living room. They sat down on the couch as he explained what she wanted so badly to understand. He admitted to sleeping around with her sister three times. One of those three times, she got pregnant with Jordan. All three times took place in the same year. His guilty conscience would not allow him to continue with the affair.

Jamie listened as he continued to give her explicit details of his shortcomings. Most things were hard to stomach. Jamie found herself swinging and punching her husband at times. The thought of him creeping into her little sister's room while she worked overnights was enough for her to shoot him dead. When Jordan got conceived, her sister, Kimmel, was eighteen, almost nineteen years old. Karl, at that time, was supposed to be her thirty-four-year-old uncle, not her partner in a one-night, well, a three-night stand. "You should feel real nasty right about now." She told him.

"I do. In the end, Jamie, I love you and want to raise our baby together as a family, but I am unsure how to move forward. I am almost positive trust will always be an issue, and you will not look at Jordan the same."

"For the last time, Jordan is innocent. I will cut Kimmel and you before I ever hurt my nephew. Jordan is my heart. I raised him right along with Kimmel and you for the last six years of his life. No one is going to take that from me. The sad truth is that he will have to learn that his baby cousin is also his sibling due to his nasty mother and horrible uncle slash father when he gets older. Disgusting!"

"You are right, and that will sound bad to him." Karl agreed, shaking his head.

"I do not know why I am sitting here crying over a man like you. I can do better than this, and I know it. You're right. You do need to move with your mother for a while. But…you will never gain full custody of our baby. Just wait until the judge hears about your unfaithfulness."

"So, are we getting a divorce now? Right to the courthouse, there is no separation or time to think things through, huh?"

"Did you think about all that while having fun with my little sister? She was young and naïve, and you self-took advantage of a child."

"You know what, I will not go there with you. I will grab some clothes and leave while there is still a little peace." He got up from the couch. "And for the record, your sister might have been young, but she knew what she was doing. Kimmel does hate you. Your mother, Cena, does too. They all hate you because of your arrogancy. You are too much. See you in court!"

Meanwhile, Casanova searched Wren's house, calling out her name. In her art lab is where he found her designing a new line. "What's going on?" he asked, confused about the divorce filing. He held the papers in the air.

"Casanova, calm down alright," she asked, feeling the anger fuming from his soul.

"I cannot calm down. Here we are, taking steps towards forever, and you are smiling in my face and filing papers behind my back. Am I that bad of a person to you?"

"Those words are very familiar, and the slap to my face normally comes right after that." Wren reminded him.

"Wren, I have not raised my hands at you since you have been out of the hospital. I prayed, studied my actions, prayed again, rebuked that Spirit, and studied. I believe God has removed that spirit of control from me.

I need you to stop reminding me of who I was and allow me to be who God has called me to be."

Wren stood speechless. Those words penetrated her soul. God is a healer; if a person allows him to move in their life, he can heal and deliver. She thought, *who am I to judge?* Then, another side reminded her not to be his test. Each time Casanova fails, she will receive the punches. He would have to repent and fight to get stronger in deliverance. Who knows how long complete restoration could take for him? It was something about her that angered him to the core. If he does not work on his flesh daily, he could punch her and repent for the next ten years. In her mind, time apart and in separate homes would be the best approach to save their marriage.

Casanova left the art lab. He was reminded in spirit that the battle was not his but the Lord. If Wren were not ready to work and trust God with him, they would fail in this union anyway. He grabbed a few more items he had left behind in their bedroom.

Wren joined him. "Casanova, I am making this decision for peace. I enjoy the peace and quietness around my home. I love not having to walk on eggshells trying to please you. I feel great when you are not around because I can have an entire day without being degraded by you. I love the peace. And every time I think about working things out with you, I feel a heaviness, a depressing feeling. I do not serve a God of misery and confusion. I hate that I stutter over my words with you, cannot think straight, and am scared. I do not think that life is for me."

"That life is not for either one of us. If you think that makes me feel great as a man that my wife is scared of me, it does not. Who wants controlled love? God does not even want controlled love. God has all the power to make us love him, serve him, and do whatever he wants us to do. Instead, he allows us a choice. He wants us to choose to love him because we want to and not force it. The love you described sounds forced. I do not want you to stay with me if that is how you feel. I set you free to choose wisely and be happy again."

"If you genuinely mean that, then allow me my continued space. I will stop the divorce proceedings to re-kindle what we had initially. We can date each other again and not rush into moving back together."

"That sounds hard, only because we are already married. But if dating in separate homes is needed much longer, I take it over a divorce."

"Thank you, Casanova!" Wren smiled, extending her arm to shake hands.

"You are not welcome, Wren, but understood." He half-smiled back, shaking her hand in agreement. Casanova's goal was to come over and win his wife back in total, not partially. He encouraged himself to accept what was given as he was not in control; God was.

Steven and Wren met at their mother's Sharon house for breakfast the following day. Wren personally thanked her for being there while hospitalized. She finally felt the push in her heart to make amends.

Sharon's home smelled like salmon patties, rice, and homemade biscuits. Wren's favorite childhood breakfast. Steven missed his mother's cooking and remembered it like yesterday. They sat at the table and said grace before devouring their food.

"Sharon, well, mother. Again, thank you for being there for me at the hospital. My husband told me you were the glue that kept everyone together while I rested." Wren began, wiping her mouth with a napkin.

"Wren, there is no need to thank me for what I am supposed to do, be a mother. I apologize for making the biggest mistake: choosing a drug deal prison term over taking care of my children. Those drugs were not mine, and I was stupid to take the deal for Daniel."

"Yes, you were mother, but we all make mistakes. When I decided to marry Casanova, it was not long before I discovered I had made a mistake. I must live with those consequences just as you have to live with yours."

"No, you do not have to live with that dude, Wren," Steven said. "All you have to do is say the word, and he'll come up missing quickly and not on my watch either." Steven snapped.

"Steven, the man she married, is a pleasant gentleman. His parents spoiled him much, and he's accustomed to getting his way. However, Wren is my creation, and she will not be an easy pushover. That frustrates poor Casanova, so he fights and swings like a little spoiled kid, hoping to get his way."

"Mother, why does that describe him so well?" Wren asked, taken back by her mother's wisdom.

"I have been gone for a while, but I am not slow by far—I heard about his upbringing. I did my research on the big actor. The man barely had to tie his shoes. That mother of his is an overprotective scary looking clown. All I can say is, Wren, let God lead you. If he leads you to stay with that man, he will fix the issue. God warns us before destruction. Take note and choose wisely. Godly!"

"Wow! That was much to take in but thank you. I feel led in my Spirit to endure. Not for personal reasons, but for the assignment. Casanova's and I union are more important than us."

"All you must do is keep praying. God will make it clear. Wait on Him and trust him." Sharon rose from the table to clear it and load the dishwasher.

"So, are you back with Daniel?" Wren asked her.

Sharon closed the dishwasher door and started it. She looked over at her adult children, unsure how to explain what they needed to know. They deserved to know the truth, and she was tired of hiding the details. "No, I am not with Daniel. He picked me up from prison," she started.

Wren could tell by her mother's expression that there was more to say. Wren smirked at her. "Did he have any intentions of getting you back?" she asked.

"No, well, yes! Daniel divorced me and cut me off when I was behind bars. I had no one to help me find you two. No one would deal with me because I decided to love a man over loving my own. Daniel picked me up from prison and gave me a lump sum of money to help me get into this place. That was the least he could do for me. He did not have to serve time for a crime he committed."

"True, but I thought Steven told me you two got back together."

"Daniel left that woman he married the second he found out I was up for release. He told me the woman could never measure up to me or what we shared. He wanted a do-over, and I settled for a moment. "

"Just like that, huh. How could you fall for that after spending time behind bars and losing your children?" Wren questioned.

"Exactly, that is why it was short-lived. While behind bars, I developed a relationship with Yah, as most know as God. I discovered who I am. I prayed for years, cried, grew, and had faith and determination never to be that vulnerable woman again. I told Daniel there was nothing left in me, no love here. I lost my children, my life, and many years to a man who ran off with a woman before I could settle in the cell. He placed no money on my books, cut me off, and threw my children to the wolves. And no matter how much Daniel claimed to love God and that he was a changed man. I could not trust it."

"I needed to hear that, mother. Thank you for that!" Wren got up from her chair and hugged her mother tightly. At that moment, healing began.

Sharon sat Steven and Wren back down at the kitchen table without hesitation. She began to pour knowledge into them. Wren was a glue to the thoughts her mother shared as they aligned with what she had experienced in that coma.

Wren understood that although the struggle had been real throughout the years, everything happened for a reason. Yet there was one thing she needed to know for complete closure. "Mom, who is Steven and my father? I am sure you found out that Daniel's DNA got evaluated. Since he is not our father, can you tell us who he might be? Do we have the same father?"

"Yes, and this is the day I dreaded. Of course, I know your father, and yes, you have the same father. Your father's name is Oscar Kent."

"Oscar Kent! Why does his name sound familiar?" Wren asked, looking at Steven.

"His name does not ring a bell for me," Steven added, nodding his head.

"Wren, has Cartel ever shared the horror one of her foster parents took her through?"

"Yes, but how would you know about that?" Wren questioned her mother.

"Oscar Kent is the man who molested Cartel as a teenager. He is the monster that got her pregnant. His wife, Tonya Kent, is the animal who helped him hide it. They took her to that southside abortion clinic to terminate her pregnancy."

"Mother, you are right! Cartel told me about this after we met in college. Wait, but again, how do you know about that?"

"Wren, when I got out of prison, I started looking for a job. I got turned down by several employers because of my felony background. Susan at the Southside flower shop gave me a part-time job. Susan and I became close. And although I stopped working for her within a year for a better job opportunity, our bond remained close after discovering our daughters were best friends. I learned you moved to Naperville and that Steven was still in the South but in Hyde Park."

"This makes so much sense now, " Wren began. "And since Susan had been following Cartel's tracks all of her life, I bet she opened that flower shop on the same street as Cartel's shop to get close to her, correct?"

"You are so correct!" Sharon confirmed.

"Wow! God works in mysterious ways. You could not get a job anywhere; then you stumbled upon a job that connected you back to Steven and me." Wren retorted. "It is crazy because I did not even believe there was a God when I went into a coma. I have degraded God's name and presence since you left Steven and me. Yet, he never stopped loving me."

"Yah, Wren. Yah works in mysterious ways. Gain some knowledge. Please read up on him. He never promised us that things would be easy. Even as followers of Christ, we will go through long-sufferings as Yeshua did." Wren curiously looked at her mother.

"Yeshua?" Steven questioned. Never had he heard of such a person.

"Yes, Yeshua, who is Jesus Christ in truth." His mother reiterated.

"So, are you connected with those Black Hebrew Israelite folks? You sort of sound like those camp-based leaders." Wren asked, having heard of them beforehand from a friend in college.

"Not at all. I am a follower of the Messiah, Jesus Christ in Truth. For he is the son of Yah (God). Some, not all of us, Black people are descendants. However, being a descendant is not to get confused with an automatic pass into the kingdom."

"Interesting, tell me more, mother. This sounds familiar." Wren explained, moving her chair closer to her mother. Wren pulled out her IPAD, opening a section to take notes.

"Yes, of course. You have to understand the Old Testament and the new testament to understand the purpose of the Messiah. See, Yeshua (Jesus) intercedes with the Father on behalf of us. Yeshua (Jesus Christ) died on the cross for our sins. Therefore, working in the physical elements of law, like the camp base leaders teach, debunks the Spiritual; grace." she concluded.

"Which makes sense as to why we must not only get knowledge filled but also Spirit-filled. Now that part, I understand well. The division amongst the denominations in the churches and the Hebrew church leaders, whether camp-based or not, fight against the churches makes no sense. No wonder the world is confused. So many are unlearned. The fight should not be against each other if the common core is the Messiah."

"My points exactly, my love. In Spirit and Truth. Have you not read the bible in full yet?" Sharon asked.

"Yeah, but the Bible has contradictions. So, I do not know about that, mom." Steve interrupted in protest.

"You mean, missing books and alterations, son. Let us speak clarity regarding the word." Sharon declared.

"Of course, that is what Steven meant. I knew where he was going." Wren guarded.

Sharon discerned the defensive mechanism from Wren on behalf of Steven. "Wren, I am the mother here. You can pipe it down a bit when it comes to me. I have a love for both of you," Sharon reminded. She went on to say," the bible has alterations as in, books missing, and words changed. And although we have folks who call themselves bible scholars who teach by interpretation. One thing that could never be altered or interpreted is he that hath ears to hear, let him hear. Be careful and take heed. Pray and ask Yah to reveal the necessary. He will direct your path. He will lead you to the knowledge needed."

"My apology, Sharon. Well, mother. I still carry overprotectiveness for my brother." she acknowledged. Wren got reminded of scripture text she had read. In the Old Testament, the physical laws where humans worked hard not to sin failed many times in physical workings, offering animal sacrifices for sin. She recalled in Hebrews an unchangeable priesthood: the forevermore, Jesus Christ. The animal sacrifice got fulfilled through Christ, who offered himself. For the sins of others, once, he offered up himself. Wren looked to Steven, who had fallen to his knees in silent worship.

"Just let him be, Wren," Sharon calmly instructed. "Wren, baby. I do not even have all the answers because our history of who we are, was destroyed. The rabbit hole runs so deep. However, I researched Mr. Casanova. Did you know that his mother, Anna, parents belonged to a camp?"

"No, ma'am, I did not know that" Wren got up from her seat. She paced back and forth across the kitchen floor for a moment, hoping to brace herself for what was next. "Mom, what does that mean?"

"Well, I have been trying to understand the control mechanism in Casanova. I spent time with him when you were in that coma. At times, my knowledge got conceived as an authoritative notion. I had to ask him several times to understand that Yah also used women in the Bible. Remember Deborah, the judge. Point proved that God used a woman to execute plans and aid decision-making to free the Israelites from bondage. She called on Barak, and he accepted the call."

"So, how do Casanova's control behavior equate to women having their minds?"

"The camp his mother's parents were raised taught that women were unlearned. They should be quiet and learn from their superior male head. I discern Casanova's upbringing has much to do with his issue. He never witnessed his mother having a voice when it came to his father. I would like to speak with both his mother and father one day. Casanova is unlearned, and a conversation amongst us all will aid in his healing. And although the husband is the head of the wife, he is to get led by Christ. He is to love his wife as Christ loved the church."

"You might be right, mom. But I thought Casanova told me once it was his grandmother who taught Anna to be silent." Wren calmed herself, taking a seat back at the table. Steven rejoined them, wiping tears from his face.

Wren knew some, not all, of the Hebrew leaders taught in a discrediting way regarding the woman. She recalled a black male friend who went by a Hebrew Israelite name instead of his birth name in her college days. Wren learned from him about why the superior race of this world truly hates the Black American people. She determined truth in that regard due to the state of our condition. Other than that, the degrading of women and being taught to hate had no biblical connection.

"Yah is still in control. Wren, you, and I have been separated and taken down some paths that felt unfavored during the time. Yet, all praise The Most High for allowing us to make it through. It reconnected us as a family and all of us to him. All praises!"

"You got that right." Wren agreed.

Still baffled by God's miraculous works, Steven sat in amazement. He attests that Susan was the person who connected his mom and him but had no idea about the rest of this mystery. Today's truth made him more interested in knowing God for himself. His miraculous works show he is still on the throne.

"Mother, I do not feel the need-to-know Oscar Kent, especially if he molests children. I would never want Cartel to connect him to Steven and me." Wren voiced; getting up from the table, she walked over to a large kitchen window, allowing the sun to beam on her face.

"Mom, how did you know Oscar Kent molested Cartel?" Steven asked, still confused.

"As I said, Susan and I became close. It was not long before we started talking on a personal level. I often spoke about you two. She spoke about Cartel. She kept her ears to the street about Cartel's upbringing. When she learned that Cartel was in his care, she went to the courts to fight for her daughter but got told her rights expired at Cartel's birth, and she had no power. She had given all her rights up when she gave Cartel to her father."

"Wow, which had to hurt her bad," Steven said.

"Yes, because Susan knew from the streets about other little girls who became part of Kent's care. Have you ever noticed that huge dash on Susan's head?"

"Yeah, Cartel and I made joking comments about that dash a time or two," Wren admitted, facing her mom and brother.

"Yeah, but Cartel does not know it was because Susan went to Kent's home and fought Tonya Kent to free Cartel. Foster parents have it easy. They quickly get these children in their care for the gain of money and abuse them in ways no one could ever imagine. And the lazy, and I say it with emphasis, "lazy" workers assigned to these cases miss every key detail. Most are there for a paycheck, not because they want to protect children." Sharon made it clear.

"Wren and I had foster parents to watch closely, but we did not undergo rape and physical abuse. Sheena, one foster mother of ours, introduced Wren to stripping for money. Other foster parents might have verbally abused us, but nothing close to what Cartel endured, " Steven confirmed. Steven got up from the table and met Wren, deep in thought, near the window. "Are you ok, sis?"

"Not at all, Steven! Cartel is my best friend. She struggles to stay pregnant, her marriage is rocky, and we share the same blood with the culprit who caused her misery. We are the product of this nasty child molester! How do I support my friend from now on with this information haunting me?"

"I know. I hate that nigga for her." Steven spoke in anger.

"Steven, do not say that street stuff around me. We are Black people and do not honor the "N" word." Wren corrected him.

"Yeah, ok," Steven smirked.

"Ok, mother, I promise this is my last question. How did you marry Daniel but have two children with Oscar?" Wren walked up to face her mother, seated at the table.

"Oscar was the big man supplying the drugs to Daniel. I was already pregnant with you when Daniel and I started messing around about a month into my pregnancy. Daniel knew you might have been Oscar's daughter; he confided that he could not have children. Oscar and I continued to mess around for years, even after Daniel and I married. Daniel felt he could not have children, but he believed God miraculously blessed him when we got pregnant with Steven. Daniel was a great man, a man of faith. He also had a heart for fast money. Daniel never thought in a million years that I would cheat on him. He treated me like a queen, and I was not about to lose out on the opportunity of my children having a great father. I shielded the lie."

"That is some story you have there, mother. I agree; Daniel was a great father. I was daddy's little girl. He took loving care of Steven and me until that woman convinced him to DNA assess us. But at least now, I can understand the hurt and betrayal he felt when he learned the truth, but he should never have taken it out on Steven and me," Wren responded. "I hated him, which started my onward hate for all men. I could not trust after losing a father that I loved so deeply, I could not trust."

"I agree with Wren," Steven co-signed, walking over to their mother. "I feel like you owe Daniel an apology too. You cannot push all this on him. Yes, you took the case for him that separated you from your family, but you made this man think God blessed him with his children. Do you understand how heartbreaking that can be for a man who wants to father children?"

"Right," Wren added. "He cut you off because he was full of pain as well. He would not have cut you off if he did not learn that awful truth. He would have continued to provide for Steven and me and provided for you in the system until you came home."

"I agree with my sister. And although it was still stupid for you to take the case for him, you are much to blame as he, mother. You need to own your faults and forgive him for his." Steven ended.

In deep thought about all of this, Wren moved to the living room, followed by Steven. Here she battled her husband, Casanova, who understood his demon and put forth a daily fight for restoration. He understood his wrongdoings and begged for a chance to prove himself. However, her mother was a selfish creature with a man still fighting to win her back after deliberately lying to him about birthing his children. She noted when a man loves. He loves hard.

"What are you thinking about?" Steven asked, taking a seat on the couch with her.

"You know what, bro? I remember the first year when Cartel and George opened that salon. Remember when I told you I ran into Daniel, and by the look on his face, I could tell he wanted to say something to me."

"Yep, I remember that, and I told you to forget that punk. I told you that he was wrong to abandon us and was only reaping what he had sowed."

"Yes, I remember, but even though I heard your words, bro, something told me it was more to that story. I just let it go, and now we learn from our mother the truth."

"So, what now?" Steven asked.

"Well, I forgive mom, and I also forgive Daniel. They both were a sad case of nothing at one point. Dealing with drugs was one thing but lying about your children's identity is another emotion. I am grateful to God for allowing us to get through it all. It was part of our journey for a reason; all we can do is forgive and continue to trust God."

"But what about Cartel? How do you look her in the face and know your father molested her?"

"I am so scared of that truth, bro. I never want to lose my best friend and sister, Cartel. She has been through so much. Her story is worse than ours. I must pray and ask God for the best timing to share this awful discovery with her."

"That's facts," Steven agreed, hugging his sister.

At that moment, Wren received revelation. All of the unknowns became known, and her purpose got defined. While she sat with her brother, Steven, he took another shot at degrading Casanova. He reminded Wren that Casanova broke his word to take care of her, allowing him a green light to act on his default.

Wren did her best to ignore her brother's ill feelings toward her husband. She reminded herself that this was the time to keep family out of their marriage. She wished Steven never discovered or was brought into Casanova's downfall. Hearing how badly Steven wanted to murder him was hard to digest.

Sharon joined her family in the living room. She sat next to Wren on the couch. Wren appeared flustered after listening to Steven's rant about Casanova. "Are you ready to leave, Wren?"

"No, ma'am, I cannot eat and run. I am here to enjoy time with you as well."

"Good, because I have one last thing to say to you both. Steven, allow me to speak about your situation. I want to encourage you to stop wasting your girlfriend, Shai, life. If you are into that woman, marry her. If you are not, let her fly. Every time I see you two together, she barely hangs in there. Not in; you are mistreating her, meaning she wants more. She is worth more but is settling by waiting on you."

"You do not think I am her type?" Steven asked.

"She is not your type, son. That woman is looking for something you are not ready for at this point in your life. One day you will see it and agree with me. Do not make any decisions off my perception, though; pray and think for yourself. Yah will strengthen you to get in position or pour into you to let her fly."

I understand your point already. I've gathered the same impression over the years. I will think more about it." Steven told her.

And as for you, Wren. Do not let your friends tell you how to oversee your marital affairs. Marriage is the highest relationship after Yah. You cannot treat something Yah has brought together as regular. It needs protection at all costs, even from close family and friends."

"So, what are you saying, mother?" Wren asked, slightly confused.

"Deep inside, you know your husband. He has a control problem and admits that. It is up to you to decide if you will work with him, keep the faith, or walk away. Whichever you choose, make sure it aligns with Yah and not lean to your understanding or unwillingness to endure for the greater purpose. Remember Yah allows us to go through some things we do not understand, but all glory is to him. Whatever he does with Casanova and you, he will get the praise in the end."

"Understood," Wren responded, rising from the couch. She explained that she needed to leave. She had prayers lifted and awaited God's direction.

'Understood, but before you go, Wren, please know that I did not have to raise you to know you. You are my daughter. It is written all over your face. I just want Casanova and you to make it. There is something inside of me that roots for you two."

"Yeah, let me go on that note. Half of me cannot understand why you would root for a man who abuses me whenever he loses his temper. I do not believe God approves of his actions. I am not his slave, and he cannot just treat me that way. Then, another part of me hears you loud and clear for some strange reason. I just need to go!" Wren announced again.

"And that is exactly why I encouraged you to seek Yah. I am delighted to have Steven and you back in my life. I prayed for this while in prison and during the many years, I have been out. Forgiveness is everything. Maybe once you forgive Casanova and let go, you will overcome."

"Agreed. I agree with you, and thanks again for inviting me over. I am sure we will have more conversations in the future." Wren grabbed her things, heading out the door.

Broken7

In her car, her mind shifted, thinking about designer project deadlines, her marriage with Casanova, and the thought of having children. She hadn't told him or anyone yet that she was expecting their first child. Speaking to Cartel about it would be bittersweet, as she'd been praying years for a baby. And now, the news that her father could be the why Cartel could not bring forth a child could be more painful and harmful to their relationship.

Wren thought, telling her brother would be a complete waste. He hated the thought of Casanova. She then imagined how Casanova would react to the news; he would instantly become overprotective and just too much. And last, Casanova's mother, Anna, would have Wren come up missing. *Actor Casanova Bryant's wife was mysteriously found dead.* She could see the headlines now. *She got eaten by a lion or something.*

Her mind shifted again to the thoughts of Garcia and the fact that she was planning to marry her best friend in less than two months. Now that she understood the word and why Cartel stood against it. She wanted to help Cartel find the right words to stop Garcia's madness. And last, there was Jamie, who she needed to catch up with to ensure all was well. She missed her call last night and still had not found the time to call her back.

Wren pulled up to her home, her mind still running in several directions. Her phone rang, and she answered. Jamie was screaming hysterically through the phone. "Wren! Wren, they found Kimmel. She hung herself!"

"Wait, in jail?" Wren asked, confused as to what was going on.

"No, my silly mom bailed her out of jail only to leave this girl frantic over possible jail time, and she killed herself!" Jamie explained, sniffing, and crying.

"Huh?" Wren tried to comprehend. "But she would not have gotten jail time. No one was severely hurt. I am super confused. Are you at home?"

"Yes, I am home. My sister is gone, Wren. I never got to make amends. She died hating me for a reason I will never know, now!"

"Calm down. I am on my way to your house." Wren informed her, backing out of her driveway.

Chapter Six: Goodbye Yesterday

The funeral was challenging for all the ladies and their husbands. It brought them together in love and support for Jamie, the twins, Jordan, and Karl. However, not much sympathy got offered to Cena, who blames Jamie for her daughter's death.

The friends met at Jamie's house; Casanova and George sat with Karl downstairs in his old man cave. They understood Karl's position and wanted to offer unbiased support. Karl had made it clear that he wanted his wife back after reconsideration. However, Casanova nor George could find the right words to support Karl now. They understood from their wives' perspective that Jamie was done. And after her sister's passing, she was at a point of no return. Karl handed the men soda cans. He flipped on a sports channel and made himself comfortable in a lazy boy chair.

Casanova twisted off the lip of the can cap, taking a sip. He needed to start a conversation but was unsure where to start. He later asked, "Karl, where do you see this thing going from here?"

Karl silenced the television. "Man, this is the stuff you see in movies. You would never think a person's real life could be this way. I slept with my wife's sister out of insecurity. And at this point, I do not care how I sound as a man. I do not care how weak it makes me look. It is my truth."

"Help me to understand that, though, bro. I am never here to judge. We men are always so caught up in not looking weak that we hide our feelings. I just want to hear you out." Casanova asked.

"Look at Jamie; she is super fine, intelligent, and does not need or want or anything. In her own right, she is that girl. Any man would love to have that independent queen on his arm, correct? That dime chick, trophy wife."

"Yeah, I agree with that point. She is fine and has her own, but what does that have to do with the heart? Or who she is as a person?" Casanova questioned.

"I could not find my place with her. She raised her siblings, put herself through college, purchased a home, became a nurse, and is amazing. However, I felt last on her list. I found myself begging for her attention. I know I was as successful as she, but I almost envied that woman. I felt ignored; she never was available for me, for us."

"You mean, you did envy. You cannot ALMOST envy someone. Either you envy the person, or you do not. My question is, why envy her? You just said you are just as successful."

"It was not the success factor; she did not acknowledge me. I felt I gave my all to her, but she never acknowledged anything I had accomplished. She showed appreciation, cooked, cleaned, and had a sexual relationship, but I needed more. She was not there for me like I needed her to be. I needed her to tell me I was a great man and the best thing, but she never did. And it was not on purpose. I just did not know how to explain what I needed. So, I gave up because I felt she did not care and found a way to hurt her deliberately."

"Man, I am not trying to make you feel some way, but this is the dumbest stuff I ever heard. It is not the part about you feeling ignored either, " Casanova began. "Dude, this woman had to be a mother to her siblings. She never had time for herself. Here you are, as her husband, not getting what you need from her, so you cheat with her younger sister to hurt her? The cheating with the younger sister part is what I find as a stupid decision."

George stepped in. "No, Casanova, you missed this brother's point. This man was weak in his spirit from something that had nothing to do with his wife. He could not understand what he needed, so he could not explain it to her. So, she did not get it. And after begging her for something he could not explain, it weakened him more. To the point of rebelliousness, he then seeks to destroy her. Why? Because he started feeling like she was too much. She was cocky, strong, and better than others. He wanted to bring her high horse down to size, hurt her, and make her feel that he was feeling neglected. However, Jamie is nothing like that. And this man knows that now. His issues stimulated elsewhere, but Jamie suffered the blow."

"My point exactly, George," Karl confirmed, pointing his finger in George's direction. "Man, I hated how strong my wife was and that she never allowed anything to bring her down. She succeeded through any battle. Why was I not that strong? Yet, I struggled with that from my mother. As a child, I used to compete with my sister. It was like, I could win a certificate for being the best basketball player, and my mom would smile and kiss me on my forehead and say an excellent job. Yet, my sister or even my younger brother could win the same reward, and she would tell the world about it. We would celebrate over dinner because she would be so thrilled, and I used to be like, why wasn't she that happy for me? I won an award too."

"Then you meet your wife. Who reminded you of your mother? Strong, beautiful, and would hug and kiss you on the forehead for your accomplishments, but broke the bank celebrating her or her siblings, correct?" George added.

"Case and point, you get it, George. And as a man, I did not want to sound like a girl begging attention. I told myself to man up. Then her little sister became an adult and started flirting with me. When I got that last award, she waited until her sister went to work that evening. She busted into our room with the most expensive bottle of wine, cards, money, and

Broken7

balloons and said, " You did that, Karl. Let us celebrate!" And I do not think she meant for it to go as far as it did, but the appreciation was it for me."

"Now, that part. I cannot help you with man. Nothing in me agrees with that outcome," George made clear. "But I do understand your pain and position."

Casanova sat quietly and took note. He recollected his thoughts and understood that families have a lot of brokenness. Many relationship issues are more profound than the attack on each other. It could very well be the product of the environment. "Man, I just realized we are some products of the environment. Everyone knows what they have got taught and what they've endured. Yet somewhere, we must take ownership and change based on what is right." Casanova mentioned.

"Yeah, but how do you know what is right or wrong all the time?" George asked.

"It'll take something or someone to teach you right. I did not know I was treating Wren wrong. My mother is a different woman who worshiped my dad's feet. So, I got raised to believe that the man is the head, and the wife is the obedient enslaved person. Then realized Wren could not adapt to that. She was stronger than most women, and I started tripping. I was going to make her obey me. I was the head. She better recognized my authority, so I thought. Then when I almost lost her, I started asking God to show me who I am. Show me who I am supposed to be and how I look in his eyes. I got a rude awakening in my spirit, bro."

"Yeah, and I can say the same thing about Jamie. I hurt her, and I told her I did not love her, then all she wanted to know is where she went wrong and what she could have done better?"

"Wow! Now that is a strong woman!" Casanova shook his head, amazed.

"Yeah, but that was short-lived; she then switched up and said she is better than that, and she is done and has not changed her mind yet."

"I mean, would you forgive her? If she had a baby with your brother living in your house. Then after so much confusion and fighting with your brother for reasons unknown, he commits suicide. Her sister died with guilt, confusion, and the thought of jail time. She felt low about facing her son after all this craziness. She could no longer ingest it, so she ended her life." George explained, rising from the couch. It bothered him thinking about how miserable Jamie's little sister must have been.

"I think I would have eventually forgiven Wren, but I would divorce her. The trust got broken, and the humiliation would be unbearable. The marriage covenant got broken." Casanova noted.

Karl rubbed his hand across his forehead. He knew the fellas were correct in their thoughts, but how he wished this were not the reality. His son, Jordan, lost his mother due to guilt from the betrayal that was so powerful. Now he is left to raise him; he would have to explain the history to his son one day. On top of that, he will grow to love a sister, his first cousin. And last, his favorite aunt, Jamie, only God, knows how their relationship would end.

The men continued to converse, sharing their downfalls, watching sports, and chuckling a time or two before heading back upstairs to the women. Karl was grateful for the knowledge the brothers poured into him. He fought the battle of being acknowledged for years. After talking with the guys, he respected his wife's decision to part ways. His new goal was to work on himself and become a better man.

Casanova identified some things about himself as well. He, too, was grateful for the time shared with George and Karl. He learned it was ok to put down the tough guy's image and that controlling a woman was not Godly intended. He was grateful to be held accountable for his actions but not condemned. He committed to himself to do better for himself, not for Wren.

After sharing details about what led to almost losing his wife, Cartel, even George had shameful feelings. He acknowledged the brothers for allowing him a place of vulnerability to be authentic. The brothers knew Black men were strong by nature, but even the most muscular men needed a space to admit fear, failure, and wrongdoings. The men understood that evening they were not weak to vent out frustrations. It did not take away their strength but began building them up and improving them as men.

After giving fist-pumps, they returned upstairs to their wives.

The ladies were enjoying glasses of wine and conversation. They sat at a dining room table surrounded by snacks, wine, and tissue boxes. A few tears became evident based on the volume of balled-up tissue next to them.

"You all good up here?" Casanova asked. He looked to Wren.

"All is well." Jamie beamed at him, giving the thumbs up to Wren.

"What's that some type of code or something?" Casanova mocked the thumbs up, laughed, and pushed Wren's shoulder as he stood behind her.

"No, Casanova, I am tired. I told the ladies I was about to go downstairs to let you know I am heading out." Wren responded.

"That is cool. I am ready to head out as well. Can I walk you to your car?"

"Yes, and I would like you to follow me home. We need to talk."

Casanova grinned so widely. His eyes lit up, looking up to God, hoping this would be a talk of restoration. He was tired of living in separate homes. He helped Wren from her chair and waved goodbyes to their friends.

"Yeah, I think George and I will follow their lead. It has been a sad day for all of us. Jamie needs time to rest. Well, at least try to rest." Cartel acknowledged.

"I agree. I am a little sleepy. Thanks for being there for me, Cartel, and George. I appreciate you both."

"No thanks, needed," George responded, helping Cartel up from her chair. Cartel gave Jamie and Karl hugs as she and George parted ways.

"Jamie, may I stay the night in our home with you?" Karl asked.

"No, that will not be necessary, Karl. I am ok. I am."

"Listen, I am ok with the divorce. But I am not ok with losing you as my friend. I disrespected you to the fullest and am responsible for what happened. And the last thing I will do is keep running from it. I am staying here tonight as your support and friend. Jordan is with my mom. I have no other place to be than with you."

Jamie had no response. She smiled at him before leaving him alone in the dining room.

About a week later, after work one Friday, Wren, and Cartel met up in a Chicago suburb, Bolingbrook. They sat down to eat at a soul food restaurant. Wren regularly ate there since it was close to Naperville, but this was Cartel's first experience.

The ladies had not spoken on the phone outside of good morning text messages and a few other notes throughout each day. Wren was at a place of wanting to share her pregnancy news with her friend. She did not like withholding the information.

After the ladies finished their meals, they sat back at the table, fat with tight stomachs. Wren managed to get through ordering and eating their meals without sharing her pregnancy news. She wanted to be sure her friend was in an excellent place to receive it, and now was the best time. "So, Cartel. I have something to share with you?"

"I have something to share with you, too," Cartel responded with a massive smile on her face.

"Girl, with that huge smile, I need you to give me the news first. I am excited to know."

"I am excited for you to know Wren. George and I are pregnant again, and this time, if the baby does not make it. We are going to hire a surrogate. I learned that my eggs are fine. It is me that has trouble carrying my baby to full term."

"Yass, girl! I am so excited for you too. See, God is good. I feel like this baby is going to make it full term. This hardship you two just experienced will bond you closer; watch and believe it! All praises to Yah will be flowing from the delivery room."

"I feel that way too. And so does George for some reason, but go ahead. Share your news." Cartel smiled at her.

"I am also pregnant. And I am feeling good about it."

"What? That is awesome, but are you staying married to Casanova?"

"Of course, I am. Casanova found out the night we left Jamie's house. Talk about a grown man crying. This man hugged me so tight. He made me put my feet on the bed and told me not to move a muscle. I knew he would be overprotective, and he will do the most."

Cartel laughed aloud. "Yes, I can see Casanova being a pain in the butt, but one thing is sure. He loves you. He just needs to learn how to treat you."

"He is learning that part too. He is something different already because of his praying, counseling sessions, more prayers, and his time with my mother."

"Yep, he just did not know. So, will you be able to keep your career too?"

"Yes, he told me that he has no issues with my career goals, but if there is any proof of physical breakdown from me trying to balance it all, he will hope that I chose him and the baby over the career," Wren explained.

"And that is fair. We must keep our bodies, which are our temples, well-balanced."

"So, you never told me how things went at your mother's house that day." She brought it to Wren's attention.

"I did. I told you it went well." Wren responded, a bit uncomfortable. Hoping this was not the time to discuss her father, Oscar Kent.

"Yes, but you had a question at one point about who your father was, remember? You were going to ask her about him."

"I did. And not only that, but we also learned the truth about Daniel. He was a great guy in a tough situation, and I had to forgive him."

"Well, that is some growth. I did not expect to hear that from you." Cartel acknowledged.

"Yes, indeed. Let us get out of here." Wren encouraged, still trying to escape from the awkwardness.

"Sure, " Cartel agreed, getting up from the table. As they made their way to the parking lot, she hugged Wren and whispered in her ear, "I know your father is Oscar Kent."

Wren pulled away from her to study her friend's face. Wren was unsure if she fell into a dream or if Cartel just said what she thought. "Wait, how did you know that?" she then asked.

"No, how long would you attempt to live without telling me?" Cartel questioned.

Wren lowered her head. She could not face Cartel at the moment. Finding the right words became an instant challenge. *How do you say that to someone you care about, especially a best friend?* Wren shook it off, raising her head to face Cartel.

"You don't have to be ashamed, Wren, " Cartel teared. "What he did to me has nothing to do with Steven and you. You two are my family; however, your father is a monster."

Tears rolled from Wren's eyes; this was an actual test of their sisterhood. They had been friends since college. They had endured so much together, but nothing like this last year. They met and reconnected with their mothers. Their husbands both disappointed and hurt them to the core. Friends around them have pushed and called upon them to be there when they could barely be there for themselves. Yet, learning that your birth father molested your best friend was enough to break them. "I am so, so, sorry, Cartel!"

"For what? You had no idea. And I know you hate him just as much as me right now."

"Yes, I do, and Steven too. I don't even care to meet him. I am so good without him in my life. Cartel, I still want to know who told you that." She said, wiping her tears with a napkin.

"You must've forgotten. I also met up with my so-called mother, Susan. She finally spoke the remainder of her truth. She also spoke to that big dash on her forehead," Cartel, busted out with laughter. An inside joke Wren and she kept about Susan.

Wren laughed, "How did it come up? He is, my dad?" she added, removing her smile.

"Did you not know?" Cartel asked.

"Yes, I knew. My mother sat Steven and me down and told us the truth about everything. I would have brought it up to you, but it was too much Cartel. I was waiting for the right time."

"There is no right time, Wren. That is the type of news you deliver because there is no time better than the other. I must accredit God for helping me heal from that trauma over the years. God has allowed me to hear his name and feel nothing but sadness for his soul.

When God gets through with him, the rotting in hell is his life sentence."

"Amen to that, sis! And I hope he burns too. He is disgusting!" Wren agreed.

"You know that Garcia wants to speak with us tomorrow, right?" Cartel changed the subject.

"She wants to speak to me. I mean, me too?" Wren questioned. She was not aware of that. Garcia was close to both women but knew to tread lightly with Wren.

"Yes, she texted me earlier and said she's been feeling some way and wants to go to breakfast."

"Yeah, let me check on that because tomorrow is Sunday, and I promised my hubby a good breakfast in the AM," Wren explained, looking at her cell.

"It is cool. It is short notice; Garcia will understand. And Wren, just know I meant it when I said all is well. Make sure you let Steven know that as well."

"Will do, Cartel!" Wren hugged her, then parted ways.

Later that night, Liza and Henry Stallings met at George and Cartel's house for a date night. Cartel-cooked fish and spaghetti. She fed them dinner and pulled out the old board game of monopoly. It was good times and laughter for the group until Liza's brother sent her a text message; it was a picture of Henry. Her facial expression changed from happy to sad. She clicked on the news article to read more.

Cartel, noticing a change in Liza's nature, "Is everything ok?" she asked.

"Henry, is this you?" Liza showed him her cell phone. A prison mugshot of Henry, attached to a news article, a fugitive. The report dates back five years ago. "Are you running from the law?"

Henry glanced at the picture. He did escape prison several years ago, but he had been out of the spotlight after changing his identity. His real name on the photo read Oliver Stickmen from Charlotte, North Carolina. "See, I can explain," he began.

"Explain what?" Liza interrupted. She took his short response as a guilty charge. "So, your online dating profile did not have a picture because you did not want to blow your cover, correct? I get it now. So, Oliver Stickmen, wow!" Liza, was now hurt and embarrassed at the same time.

"Wait, is she serious, bro? Are you a fugitive? Man, why did you bring that mess to this house?" George asked him, getting upset. "Who sent you that picture, Liza?"

"My brother. When I told my family I fell in love with this intelligent Black man, they hated the idea. My brother felt from the time he met Henry something felt strange."

"Your brother is racist, and your family is racist. Of course, it would feel strange to them." Henry indicated.

"Stop it, Henry!" Liza yelled, jumping up from the table. "I went against my family for you, and you are running from the law?"

"Ah, are you a killer, bro?" George asked, wanting to know who sat across the table from him.

"I am not a killer; however, I did make a mistake. I engaged in a self-defense case where I injured someone to incapacitation. The law enforcers did not acknowledge my actions as self-defense. I received a class F felony and was sentenced to 36 months in prison. One day, the prison had a bad fire. Several of us were able to escape. I knew people. They helped me to get to Illinois, where I changed my identity. I have been fine, blessed, going to church and a changed man."

"We must call the police," Liza demanded, snatching her cell phone away from Henry.

"Wait, Liza!" Henry asked, jumping up from the table. He tackled Liza to the floor in pursuit of her phone. After grabbing it, he fled quickly from their home.

"You two just sat there and let him wrestle me over my phone. Why didn't you call the police? Is that what your Black people do, cover for each other?" Liza hollered at them.

"Your Black people!" Cartel yelled back at her. "Do not disrespect me in my home like that. We deal with that enough on the streets, and you will not do that here."

"Cousin, you let him tackle me!" Liza explained, fixing her clothes as she rose from the floor.

"Liza, it happened so quickly. You jumped, he jumped, then he ran. He was after your phone. He was not trying to beat you or anything. He does not want to return to jail; that is his issue."

"I know his issue, but it is against the law to harbor a fugitive, Cartel, and George. We need to find him and turn him in."

"Liza, are you wanting him arrested because you fell in love with a criminal, or did he just perform a criminal activity in my home? Are you that upset to the point where you want the man imprisoned?" Cartel quizzed.

"Yes, because he wasted my time. I am a professional primary care provider. I am a law-abiding citizen. He falsified his online profile and lied about who he was because of his criminal status. He stole my heart, and I do not particularly appreciate how I feel now. That said, he needs to get punished. I am calling the police on him."

"For what reason? I am still confused about what this has to do with you?" Cartel questioned again.

"I cannot get connected with the likes of him." Liza snapped.

"Look, if that man does not come back to my home or show up at my wife's and my place of business, we are not getting involved in that mess. He did nothing to any of us."

"He broke the law in another state, George. He is a criminal, and you just do not care?" Liza argued, frustrated, pacing back and forth on their floor. "Cartel, is this the type of husband you have? He harbors fugitives?"

"That is your last warning. You need to leave my house now! Talking about is that the kind of husband I have. Is that the type of man you pick up online? Ones without profile pictures are a dead giveaway; they hide stuff."

"I am leaving. I am a professional and educated doctor. I have no business dealing with the likes of you people. And Cartel, I thought the half-white part of you carried some class. I guess not."

"Girl! If you do not leave my house!" Cartel counted backward, trying to calm herself. George reminded his wife to stay calm and consider the source as he escorted Liza out of their home.

Cartel took a seat back down in a dining room chair. "George, what just happened here?"

"Bae, your guess is as good as mine. I can tell you one thing; I am tired of drama. We have gotten submerged in drama these last three to four months, and enough is enough.

"We were part of that drama at one point, George. We cannot just act like we are higher than others. The thing is - it is getting tiresome quickly. I agree with you, though. Henry's story is not our business. Black men in prison serve time for crimes they did not commit or serve maxed time for small offenses. This man has not disrespected my cousin in any way or me. She is just mad because she fell in love with a criminal. She is embarrassed, but she will get over it. Most Christians would turn Henry into the arms of the law, but because I am not sure if he committed the crime, I would rather stay out of it."

"Yeah, but a part of me wants to know if he did that crime and to whom. We might need to be turning that brother in for real."

"Well, he said he did the crime out of self-defense. He knows we are on to him, so he will not be back this way. He will not be connecting with Liza any time soon either."

George searched online via his phone. "I just found him online. It looks like Oliver Stickmen was the victim of attempted robbery. A disabled man in a wheelchair drew a weapon at Oliver. It reads that he was able to take the robber's gun and use it against him. However, instead of shooting the gun to kill the man, the pistols beat him into a coma, but he lived. If the disabled man drew a gun, how is that not self-defense?"

"I have no idea. It was the beating into a coma that was wrong. As for me, I am going to bed. Today was drama-filled, and I just need sleep." Cartel cleared the table. She had no more room on her plate to carry anyone else's battles.

Broken7

"I agree," George told her, helping to clean up after their guest.

Sunday morning Wren and Cartel met up with Garcia for brunch instead of early breakfast. Wren made sure to feed her husband before joining the ladies that morning. Garcia appeared flustered. She explained her frustrations and decision not to marry Yesenia.

Garcia also alerted that after she broke the news to Yesenia. She immediately got attacked. Garcia felt convinced that marrying a woman was not the right thing to do. But she trusted Yesenia so much, which made it safe for her to marry.

"I told you that much, " Cartel reminded her. "I told you that your liking for women was a safety method. You have never liked women in the past, and then after several failed relationships with men, you suddenly drew attention to women. I was not buying it at all."

"Well, it only scared me when it came down to almost marrying the woman," Garcia explained. "Then, after she attacked me, it confirmed abusive people can be male or female."

So, now what, are you calling off the wedding?" Cartel inquired.

"I did that already, and my parents were thrilled. They too thought I was running into the arms of a woman.'

"Yep, Wren and I struggled with giving you scripture on how this displeases God. We knew you were in love and saying things that could hurt you was not our thing. Cartel told her.

"That was not my concern," Wren disagreed. "I do not care about hurting folk's feelings regarding the truth. The truth shall set you free. Hiding biblical facts is why people laugh at the thought of the Most High nowadays. Most leaders teach carefully, hoping not to offend instead of teaching the truth. I have not found in the bible that God designed women to marry women, and men to marry men."

"But where is the sin in it?" Garcia asked, "Is it not all about love?"

"Garcia, if it is not his design, then it is not his will," Wren snapped, throwing her hands up. "Listen, you decide the standard. I am not going to sugarcoat to hide biblical instruction. The family structure points to the man as the head and the woman as his mate. It points to the union of a woman and man. Also, a parent will always love their child even when they disobey instructions. You cannot take a ride on God's love as approval to do your own thing. I could never be supportive in agreement with what is not sound."

"Yeah, but Wren, leaders teach polygamy is ok based on folks in the bible. Is it written that God condemned them?"

"And here we go! Listen to the keywords "biblical instructions" I have not seen where God's intent or message was given for folks to have wives. I understand folks feel it was allowed because it did not appear condemned, but it is evident and reinforced in the New Testament of God's intent for one man to one woman. 1st Corinthians 7, Ephesians 5:22-33, 1st Timothy 3, etc."

"Wise words, Wren." Cartel applauded. It amazes me how far you have come from not believing to believing. And not by hearsay, but word-say. I love it!"

"She is the truth, and I can feel it when she speaks. She encourages me to learn the word for myself. Thank you, Wren." Garcia acknowledged.

The ladies wrapped up their brunch with laughs and giggles before parting ways. Garcia took note that she had made the right decision. She grew a strong interest in wanting to know the Lord for herself. Convinced that if God could change Wren, he could also change her life for the better.

"Ms. Cartel, how are you?" a woman asked, standing behind her chair as she wiped down her styling chair and workstation. The salon was busy, and Cartel had just enough time to clean before her next client sat in her chair.

"Well, who do we have here? I wondered when you would come back in this shop to see Valerie after your failed shot at my marriage," Cartel half-smiled. "How are you, Trisha, and how's baby Benjamin?"

"We are well. And I did need time to prep for this day. I love Valerie; she is a great hairstylist and close friend. But even she did not stand behind my messiness."

"Yeah, she told me she had no idea about it and was against it." Cartel confirmed.

"I just came to apologize. Your husband is a great man and not a cheating man. I got so messed up over my man cheating on me; I wanted to make someone miserable."

"Wow! I know that it took all of you to say those words. Not many would admit to being a miserable, jealous, low-down, disrespectful, piece of nothing." Cartel snapped at her.

"Listen, I will own all those words except the piece of nothing part. I am somebody, and I do have class. I would not stand here today if I did not have class." Trisha pointed out.

"And, that's facts, apology accepted." Cartel acknowledged, extending her hand to shake.

"Thank you!" Trisha shook her hand. "Please let your husband know of my apology."

"He heard you. He is standing right behind you. He must have seen you come my way."

"I did," George said. "I knew you would come back here one day, Trisha, but I did not know if it would be so soon."

"Well, God is good, Mr. George. Have a wonderful day, both of you." Trisha responded, walking away.

"Are you good, baby?" George asked Cartel.

"I couldn't be better." She smiled, hugging him.

Chapter Seven: A Mother's Love

After time in prayer, allowing restoration, Cartel decided to attend a mother/daughter celebrity brunching with her mother, Susan. Wren and her mother, Sharon, joined, and Jamie, with her mother, Cena. It was a beautiful brunching and much-needed start to bonding with the mothers who had been absent in their daughters' lives for several reasons.

Losing Kimmel hit home for Cena. It hit her so hard having to face up to her mistakes, leaving her children for drugs, then aiding in jealousy of Jamie, brainwashing Kimmel to hate Jamie. Kimmel's death was brutal for her. She knew she had to change her life for the twins, Jordan and herself. She also knew that a change could not be possible without fixing it with

Jamie. Jamie's new baby girl, Karlie Jamie, was an added blessing. Cena simply adored her.

Cena spoke about her journey during the luncheon, encouraging all the mothers and daughters to love and appreciate each other. She received a standing ovation. A decisive moment was honored and accepted by all. Other women got a chance to speak, but Susan's story about her journey to find Cartel left not a dry eye in the building. She called the dash on her head a punishment for giving up her child and a badge of honor, displaying her efforts to continue the fight until conquered. Not everyone gets an opportunity to change their wrongs into right. She gave God all the praise for his grace and mercy.

However, the audience did not receive Sharon's story about her children well. Some women made negative comments, while others tried to offer words of encouragement. However, Sharon came prepared for the battle. She provided scripture and wise counsel in rebuttal. A confirmation that God had forgiven her and allowed her a chance.

The friends ended the evening super proud of their mother's efforts to make things right. Listening to them speak at the luncheon awarded more insight into their mother's journeys. Wren, Cartel, and Jamie had grown to love and honor their mothers as God wanted them to.

Cartel and George decided to spend time at home the following Friday evening. They had only a matter of weeks before their baby was due. Cartel felt grateful to God she carried the baby this far and wanted nothing more than to finish strong.

Wren, whose baby was due any day, and Casanova joined their friends for a night of movies and relaxation. And although Jamie and Karl were no longer married, they were great friends and co-parents to their three-month-old, Karlie Jamie. They joined Cartel and George at home while Karl's mother kept their children. Jamie continued to be an excellent aunt to her nephew, Jordan, and an influential mother figure on behalf of her sister, Kimmel.

A knock on the door interrupted their movie. George paused the television to answer it. To his surprise, Cartel's cousin Liza stood before him. "Well, what brings you over, Ms. Disrespectful?" George asked. Behind her stood Henry Stallings, also known as Oliver Stickmen.

"I need to talk to my cousin, George. I have not spoken to her in months, which is bothering me badly.

Also, I think she would be proud to learn a few things about my life."

George guided them to the family room. He informed him they had guests over, which did not matter to Liza at that moment. She had a pressing in her heart that this was the best time to make amends with her cousin, Cartel.

"Is this a prank?" Cartel rose from the couch at the presence of Liza and Henry. "Why are you here, Liza, and how are you standing here with Henry, Oliver?"

"I can explain…." Liza began. "First, I must apologize for the racial remarks about you and George. After self-reflection, I did come off as a racist person. It was unkind; honestly, I did not feel that way towards you. Second, discovering the news about Oliver broke me in two. I hated him, Black people, and myself, all in one. I was embarrassed because I felt better, and allowing myself to fall for things other women had fallen for made me mad."

"Please, take a seat." Cartel allowed, after learning this was a time of restoration. Liza and Oliver sat beside her. George sat next to Oliver, keeping his eyes on the fugitive as he now knew him to be.

"Wait, " Wren said. "I thought this guy was on the run from the law. I know it has been months since Cartel heard from you, Liza, but how are you two still together?"

"We are not together," Oliver corrected, looking at Liza.

"Right, we are not together, but I hope to be again one day," she responded, looking back at him. She turned back to Cartel, who sat quietly and confused. Jamie and Karl sat quietly. Jamie knew nothing about what transpired between Liza and Oliver after she walked away from him in the park that evening.

"George and Cartel, I came to apologize for not being transparent about who I was and standing before you in your home. That was not the right thing to do, and I apologize. I met with my Pastor and First lady immediately after you found out. They encouraged me and took me to the police to get escorted back to prison."

"Prison? I am so confused here." Jamie yelled out. Wait, is this the guy who was on the news? Wait, Henry Stallings from the park is Oliver Stickmen?

"Yes, I am him. And yes, to prison, ma'am. I was an escapee on the run from another state. To make a long story short, I got turned in. My Pastor and First lady not only prayed for me but hired a team of attorneys, who got my case re-opened at my expense. They believed in me and fought with me. When I got sentenced the first time, I had a public defender who did nothing for my justice."

"They never do, man." George agreed.

"Yep, but God! The clean-up in my life, the church warriors, and other people behind me fought with me. And although I had made money from business investments, I lost most while serving another three months in prison. The case is now self-defense. The paper did not report that the disabled man shot at me a couple of times before I hit him once with his gun. I did not kill him, but I knocked him out. He is alive today. Now they are looking to stick him with armed robbery with the possibility of more charges."

"Wow! Another story of God's Grace and Mercy. You would have never gotten a second chance without the Lord. I do not care how many lawyers served on your team. That was all God, the prayers of the righteous availed much. God came through." Wren told him.

"I don't doubt it," Oliver confirmed, "I give him all the praise."

"Ok, I get your freedom story, but how did you reconnect with this racist being?" George asked, pointing at Liza.

"Liza and her family were following my story. They saw the news feature me. I assume they followed me from that point on. Well, Liza did."

"Yeah, I saw the news about you too." Karl announced, "I just did not know you had any connection to the people I knew."

"Yeah, we all saw that you turned yourself in. I guess I did not follow anything after that point. But I felt Liza would have reached out sooner." Cartel mentioned, rolling her eyes at Liza.

"When Oliver turned himself in, I wrote to him in prison. After I learned all the facts of his case, I visited him. I wanted to help in any way possible as his friend. He allowed me to do so. I felt stupid for not allowing him to speak his truth in your living room that day. I got to know him better behind bars and felt the same strong feelings for him as I did with Henry Stallings. As much as I wanted to fight those feelings, something overpowered it. That something is love."

"So, what's the status of you two now?" Jamie asked, still slightly confused by everything.

"We are friends and will remain that way for the time being. If there is one thing that I learned in that cell was the power of love. I am torn between something right now, and I need to understand what is right or wrong from a biblical stance. I do not need to go into my thoughts now, but Liza and I will decide what is next for us sooner than later."

"Nope, I will tell them. He was told that he should not get involved with any woman outside of his race. Some person in prison gave him all this literature, and now he is confused." Liza told the group. She felt a strong love for Oliver. She did not believe people could only find love within their race and was determined to prove this to him.

"Well, that is a touchy story. I am not prepared biblically or feel led by God to speak to it. I try not to speak out of term." Cartel responded, looking at Wren. Cartel knew that Wren also felt it was not biblical to date someone outside your race. Wren had just spoken to this a few months ago regarding another couple. She was hoping Wren would not get involved and keep a closed lid.

But of course, Wren did not keep silent. "All I will say is to read the word for yourself and ask the Most High for understanding. Do not lean on your prison cellmate's knowledge; find the truth."

"Thank you. I plan to do just that. God brought me through a tough spot in my life; the last thing I want to do is be out of his will. A part of me does not believe your soulmate can only come from your own. I have seen some interracial couples with true commitments and long-lasting loving families. I am not a racist, and I have feelings for this woman who has been with me through this ordeal; however, she is lukewarm. I told her she switches sides, reacts, thinks about it, and later returns for me. I am not cool with that part."

"Yeah, I feel you on that, bro! Liza, either you will believe in your man and roll with him based on your feelings or stick with stereotypes and myths about the Black man," George said. "I saw how you switched up when your brother sent that mugshot. You also switched up on my wife and me. No man wants a woman who partially has his back."

"That is real talk, Liza." Jamie joined in. "I am a fan of love. It does not matter who you fall in love with but make sure it is authentic. Do not settle. I recall the day you walked away from this man in the park. The minute you found out he was black. What is different today?"

"Well, I am not defending my so-called cousin, but I know our family is brutal to deal with when it comes to dating black. My mother, Trina, went through it, so I have learned through my family's words. Yet she never gave up on my dad. Liza is battling losing her family to be with this man." Cartel concluded.

"Rightfully so, but again, she cannot be lukewarm either. Stand with Oliver or against him but do not play both sides. I could not date outside my race because no matter how much that outer person says they love me, they cannot understand me like my own," Casanova chimed in. "Also, point proven, the minute this man was in trouble, she stood against him and was ready to bring him down. Did I not hear that?"

"Yep, you heard that from me," Wren confirmed. Cartel told me the whole story.

"Yes, I did go wild on him because of hurt. I am not going to lie. I was not a fan of the Black race in general. As Cartel mentioned, our family raised us to hate you all. I do not understand the full history of their hate towards Black Americans, but when you're raised to believe all the stereotypes, you will not know better until you get to know one."

"Your cousin is Black, so you had a chance to know one. You just stopped believing the hype when you met this Black brother." Jamie added, shaking her head at the madness.

"I get it, and that's a fair statement, "Liza agreed, "but I am here now, and I am not giving up. I will show Oliver that I have his back forever this time."

"And honestly, folks. That is all I ask of Liza. Time will show me through prayer to God if she is for me or not. We do have diverse backgrounds. I have to defend my case and my walk-in life as a Black man—something she will never understand. Black women can relate more because they are a part of who we are. It is understandably so. However, it does not mean she cannot love me properly if we move forward."

"Again, just make sure the love is authentic. I have seen women from different races aim at our successful broken Black men because they can see their weakness. They say we do not know how to love and treat our men. Yet, when those same relationships turn sour, that successful Black man is cleaned out of his cash after he learns her motives were not authentic—the white judge's side with their own. You better look at these ballplayers and rappers. These women are clever, aiming at weakness to attain his heart. Have babies with them for their lavish lifestyle. So, make sure it is authentic." Jamie pointed out.

"That cannot be our story. I am a physician. I make great money, honey. I do not need his cash, ok." Liza snapped at her, rolling her eyes.

"Um, his money is a bit longer than yours. This man's story got widely displayed on television—his investments in real estate, his net worth, and more. Plus, he better file for wrongful conviction or suit in the lawsuit. Again, be careful, Oliver. I know you lost money during this mess, but your knowledge is still there to regain it."

Oliver sat, amazed at the words Jamie spoke on his behalf. She was a woman who did not know much about him, but her words were strong, and he loved how she told the truth. He smiled at her. "Thank you, my sister. I do not know your name."

"My wife's name is Jamie," Karl clarified, straightening up on the couch. He caught the flirtatious smile Oliver delivered.

Jamie smiled at Oliver, then frowned at Karl. "I am your ex-wife; let's be clear here."

"Hey, no disrespect, man. I just found Jamie's comments wise and uplifting. I am here with Liza. We came to speak our peace. We both owed George and Cartel a heartfelt apology as we disrespected their home with our problems. However, I do appreciate this entire group. You all are an awesome group of friends. It is good to see our kind successful and have healthy relationships and friendships. I applaud you all and hope I am welcomed in the future."

"You are always welcome here, man," George told him. "You have one heck of a story, and to have made it this far is nothing short of amazement. I applaud you, my brother. You stood your ground and worked on yourself to become a better man."

"Thank you, and that I will continue to do." Oliver glanced over at Jamie once more. It was something about her that caught him. Jamie saw his glare and smiled; she looked to her ex-husband Karl who did not miss a beat. She thought it was cute that he was jealous, but she was not worried about how he felt about it. They were divorced, friends, and nothing more.

Liza, too caught wind of the eyeballing shared amongst Jamie and Oliver. She turned her nose up at Jamie. She wanted her to know she made a note of the interaction. George guided Liza and Oliver out while the others gathered their belongings to leave right behind them. No one wanted to restart the movie after that conversation. It was time to call it a night.

Saturday morning was beautiful outdoors, with sunshine and warmth but not too hot. It was the perfect day in May to get out and discover. Jamie asked Karl to come by her home to watch their daughter, Karlie. She planned to meet with Cartel, Garcia, and Wren at the mall.

Karl entered the home dressed to impress with a fresh pair of Jordans, a black Jordan t-shirt, and Levi pants. He smelled good too. Jamie had not seen him dressed this way in a while. *He must be getting back to life*, she thought. He walked up and hugged her. "What's that all about?" she asked.

"Just happy to see you, my friend." He joked.

"Well, thanks; I am glad to see you as well. I gave Karlie a bottle, burped her, changed her, and laid her down. She will be sleeping for a while. Are you taking her back to your mom's house to see Jordan?"

"No, mom took Jordan to see your mother. I was going to hang out here if you do not mind and watch her until you get back."

"What if I planned on bringing a man back with me?" Jamie teased.

"Whelp, I will be waiting here to meet him." Karl's face got serious. He still wanted his ex-wife back. He knew he did not have a chance in the world as she was still grieving the loss of her sister and trying to balance the fact that her nephew was also her daughter's sibling. He thought back to the night when Henry, Oliver, smiled at his ex-wife. The Oliver twist person would not get with his ex-wife on his watch. And although the Oliver twist book character and Oliver Stickmen were not the same, the running away part made them twins. He laughed to himself.

"Karl, I will open myself up to date another man at one point. I am not there yet, but it will happen. I suggest you start making that a reality. I am a good catch; someone will appreciate me one day. Just as I know, another woman will appreciate you. I am not mad at her. You are fine enough."

"There is no other woman for me, Jamie. I am not even looking for her."

"You say that now but you looked for another woman when you got with my sister." Jamie set it ablaze.

"I am not going to allow you to take us there. We were doing great not discussing the past. I am going to the nursery to check on our daughter."

Jamie took a seat in a chair in the living room. She still had a snare of strong dislike toward Karl as she thought about his mistakes and her sister's death. In time she hoped to get to a place where they could forget about it, but today was not the day. Karl rejoined her in the living room with the baby in his hand.

"She is still sleeping, Karl. You are spoiling her." Jamie told him.

"She is mine. I can spoil her all I want. Daddy's little princess. She knows that all her daddy ever needed was love." He kissed his baby girl's forehead and hugged her tight.

Jamie sat and thought a moment. *All her daddy ever needed was love.* "Karl, what do you mean by all you ever needed was love? Are you saying I did not provide that?"

Karl sat down on the couch with his baby girl. He held her close to his chest, watching her sleep peacefully in his arms. He was her protector and wanted so badly to give her the world. Finally, he looked at Jamie, who sat awaiting his response. "Jamie, I have struggled to share this with you for years. I know you loved me. I felt it. However, something was missing. I learned over these months that it was me that had an issue. I wanted to please you so bad- to hear you say, I am proud of you. I wanted you to be happy to share my accolades and feel like I was the best thing in the world to you. I never got that from you. I never got that from anyone near and dear to my heart, not even my mother."

"Really, Karl? Did you not think I was proud of my husband? I mean, ex-husband now. Man, you are brilliant. Remember, I was the one who told you to become more significant than a physician assistant because your knowledge is brighter than that physician. I always told you how I appreciated you. What are you saying?"

"I am saying that I heard the words but did not see it in your actions. You celebrated hard when it came to your accomplishments and your siblings; however, it was simple and small when it came to me."

"Because of you, Karl. You never wanted a huge celebration. How many times did you shoot down my ideas?"

"Because all I ever wanted was to feel the sincerity from you. You had little time for me but made yourself available to everyone else."

"Why did you hold that in all this time? You should have known I would never intentionally neglect you. Yes, I got caught up in work and raising my siblings, but I would have gotten it if you said something."

"I tried, but it always ended up in an argument." The baby moved around for comfort as Karl rubbed her back.

Jamie sat for a moment, silently reflecting. It became evident as she reflected upon their past arguments due to the silliest things. He was fighting for her attention the entire time. *How could she have missed that?* She looked over at Karl as he held their daughter. Her cellphone vibrated with a text message from Wren. Wren was in labor and en route to the nearest hospital. Jamie smiled at the announcement, responding with a smiley face emoji. She was happy for her friend while sad at the news she had just received from Karl. "I am sorry I missed the memo all these years." She told him.

"And I am sorry I was not brave enough to be real with you. I was trying to be a strong man and not show any signs of weakness." Karl kissed their daughter once more.

"I love how you love our baby girl." Jamie admired, smiling as he kissed their baby girl again.

"She is a blessing from God. He knew what I needed. I love this little girl so much."

Jamie got up from her chair. "I am going to head to the hospital. Wren is in labor, so no shopping for us today. I will check on her and Casanova, then head back."

"It is cool. Take your time. I will be here with our princess."

Jamie looked at him again. She realized she had also missed Karl's love and affection at that moment. The way he held their daughter was something she had never witnessed between the two of them. She stood and watched for a couple minutes before leaving for the hospital.

Wren delivered a healthy baby boy with a C-section weighing seven pounds and seven ounces. He favored Casanova. After days at the hospital, she arrived safely home. Casanova, who was scheduled to leave out in a week for a new film, was overjoyed, in total awe. His father and mother were coming over to meet their new grandson and expected to arrive shortly.

Wren invited Cartel and Jamie over for moral support. Both ladies had already met baby Seven Bryant at the hospital, but it was Casanova's mom, Anna, who the help was needed. Jamie left her baby girl with Karl and rode to Wren's house with Cartel. Cartel wobbled in the place alongside Jamie. She was counting down the days to meet her bundle of joy.

Casanova let the women in and led them to Wren, seated on the couch in a family room. The ladies beamed at baby Seven for a moment or two before Casanova took him upstairs so the ladies could chat.

"I see that you and Casanova are doing well, right?" Cartel asked, witnessing how they interacted with each other and baby Seven. "Just one small, happy family!"

"Yes, I can attest," Wren half-smiled. "Yet, this pain is something else. I hate to use the bathroom; the cramping mechanism is unbearable. Cesarean delivery is a no for me."

Cartel sat next to Wren on the couch, with Jamie sitting next to her. Cartel silently prayed she would not end up needing a c-section. Her friend looked uncomfortable, and she was not as strong as Wren regarding pain levels. "You look well even in pain, sis!" Cartel encouraged.

"I just heard the doorbell. I know that is Anna; this is not the day for her shenanigans. I am in too much pain. She would not meet Seven this soon if I had a choice." Casanova walked passed the entryway with Seven in his hand to answer the door.

"Wren, relax. We are not going to let her talk crazy today. Not while we are sitting here with you, at least." Jamie promised.

Anna rushed into the family room holding baby Seven, followed by Gregory and Casanova. She sat down in a nearby lazy boy chair. She could not keep her eyes off him; he looked like Casanova. "I am so in love with him." She beamed.

Wren rolled her eyes at her. The sound of Anna's voice made her cringe. Anna was the devil in woman form. *How could she be so in love with Seven and dislike the mother who birthed him? She is such a fake.*

Yes, he does favor Casanova." Gregory added, gazing down at him in Anna's arm.

"Casanova, well, Wren. Why do you have company around him so soon? He is fresh out of the hospital. You have to keep outside germs away from him." She scolded, looking to Wren, then her two friends.

"I guess outside germs would apply to you too, Mrs. Bryant." Jamie reminded.

"I am his grandmother; it does not apply to me!"

"And I am a licensed registered nurse who understands germs and the body very well. You did not even wash your hands before taking him from Casanova. You just rushed right in with him already in your arms. Please do not get me started." Jamie rebuttal.

"Ok, ladies, enough is enough," Casanova interrupted. "Do I need to take my son out of this room or what? Give him peace, please."

"Casanova, do take him away from me for a moment. I want to speak to Wren alone, if I may?" Anna asked Wren. Casanova passed baby Seven to his father. Gregory.

Wren responded. "I am not feeling my best yet to get up from this couch, just to come back here with my company. Can we talk right here?"

"If we must. I openly want to apologize to you. I never gave you a fair chance from day one. I did not think you were good enough for my son. No one ever taught you how to be a wife and that it was not my son's job to do."

"Oh wait, is there a book written on being a wife?" Jamie interrupted. "If so, I need that book, Anna Bryant."

"Who are you?" Anna asked, getting frustrated with her comments and outbursts.

"A close friend of Wren's. Another professional Black woman who works hard but still is not good enough for the likes of you. Yes, I know all about you and the hell you put my friend through from day one."

"Jamie, I know you got Wren back and all, but this is my mother. Please discuss respectfully." Casanova demanded.

"I got this, bro," Jamie said, shaking her head in agreement. She placed her hand on her forehead. She reminded herself to calm down and that Anna was an elder.

"Thank you, Ms. Anna, for the apology." Wren finally responded.

"Just call me, mom. You do not have to say, Ms. Anna."

"No, Ms. Anna is appropriate, but thank you," Wren added, thinking *I would never call her fake self-mom. We have not been besties, and that will not change due to the birth of a grandson.*

"Whatever you like," Anna responded.

"Ms. Anna," Cartel called out to her. "Who taught you how to be a good wife?"

"Well, I am glad you asked, Cartel. See, Gregory's mother taught me what she learned in camp ministry. Women are to silence a man's authority and follow his lead. Your husband is your head. He is responsible for you. Even when you are unhappy with his decision, you must obey him. Continue to serve him and never disrespect him. And with that, I have been married to Mr. Gregory for about fifty years now."

"Sounds like you speak to women as a slave to her head. What bible did this come from because I have never heard of it." Cartel inquired.

"I could teach you, women, a thing or two if you allow me," Anna said, feeling inspired at the thought of teaching younger women.

"No, I do not think that is necessary, Ms. Anna. I honestly believe I could teach you a thing or two," Wren countered. "First and foremost, a woman is not the buckle down of her husband. She has a voice, and the bible speaks to women being used to conduct great plans in tricky situations. Second, those ministry camps twist the word and purposely leave out the scriptures that speak to the man having to deal with God if he treats his wife wrong. Men need to honor their wives as well. 1st Peter 3:7 Likewise, ye husbands, dwell with them according to knowledge, giving honour unto the wife, the weaker vessel, and as being heirs together of the grace of life; that your prayers be not hindered. Gain some understanding because Yah sees everything, and he is not a fan of abuse."

"Wren is biblically correct, Ms. Anna," Cartel concurred, "because you raised Casanova to believe that mess. He almost lost his wife trying to replicate. I am sorry that you got taught wrong, but I am here for it if you ever want to talk Bible."

"That sounds like a great idea," Gregory said, smiling at Cartel. Mr. Gregory Bryant sat silently in conversation, but something about bible study for Anna made him smile. He hated that his wife silenced his authority; she should have stood her ground at times.

"Gregory, why would I want to gain insight from women young enough to be my children? I am their elder; they must learn from me."

"Anna, baby, I have been praying for years that God would send you an amazing group of women in your life. And it is not because you cater to my every need and stay on my side but because you need to be around women. We have discussed that you have a voice of reason and should feel comfortable being free."

Anna squirmed in her seat. How dare Gregory discuss their conversations? Her feelings of greatness shattered. It was true, Gregory always wanted her to find herself, but she had no clue how to do just that. All she knew was working hard and taking care of Gregory and Casanova. "I will think on it and get back to you." She responded, leaving the room to wash her hands.

"That was a polite conversation, Wren. I love your intelligence. I am glad to call you my wife." Casanova acknowledged. He knew his mother had been a piece of work, but to watch how his wife managed her with respect and biblical education was admirable.

"Thank you, Casanova," Wren replied. His compliments were still hard to receive at times. Although prayer has changed things on many levels, some words still trigger negative responses.

Anna returned, taking baby Seven from Gregory. She talked baby language and hugged him tightly, taking her seat back in the chair. "So, Wren, are we in a respectable place to move forward? She asked.

"We are in a suitable place, Ms. Anna. You can sit here if you want, enjoying your grandson. Wren raised her foot on an ottoman. She was tired of the healing pain but could not help but instantly love her new son, Seven.

Jamie stepped back out in the dating world a week later on Saturday night. She met up with a man who admired her from the first time he looked at her. She brushed it off for as long as possible before saying yes to a dinner date.

After dinner, Jamie and her date went for a walk in the park. The weather was warm, a beautiful mid-seventies type of night. Laughter between her and her new guy friend alongside the park pathways was everything. Jamie never felt so giggly and alive in a long time.

"You are a funny woman. Fun to be around. I am so surprised you said yes to my dinner request and then walked in the park with me afterward; yeah, I must be winning!" Oliver smiled, giving Jamie the elbow-to-elbow hit.

"No, it was just a little weird to me at first. You were just dating Cartel's cousin, Liza. I felt the connection at Cartel's home that night, but I ignored it."

"I know. I tried to brush it off, but something kept making me think about your smile. I recalled how defensive you were, alarming me to be careful about choosing anyone as my partner. I thought that was dope. Even though you were speaking from a woman's point of view, I took it with love. That's what's up!"

"I am known to be one of the realists in the group," she responded, stopping in her tracks. "So, who taught you about the two nations."

"Wait, how did you know it was about the two nations? Liza said someone gave me information while I was in prison. She never mentioned the two nations." Oliver questioned, stopping with her.

"First of all, I am a Black, woke woman. I understood what you received. The brothers in prison have nothing more to do than educate themselves. Well, I hope that is what most are doing anyways. Do you believe in it?"

"I mean, it is evident in Genesis 25:23 and speaks to the world we live in today. So, yes, I get it. I understood it, but another thing that caused a dislike of Liza was the way she flipped sides. I could not feel confident with a woman having my back but with limits. No one will always do the right thing; we all fall short of the glory of God. I would like to have a woman who understands I am human and not just see the stereotype."

"I dig it. So, you think the flip-flopping actions were because of uncertainty?"

"Oh, for sure. She wanted to trust me, but being Black made it difficult. She was raised to believe Black people were uncaring, ruthless individuals who wanted nothing but to wreck others' lives. Her family taught them not to be friends with people like us early because we are no good folks and will have them go to jail and break the law in many ways."

"She told you all of that?" Jamie asked, curious as to why Liza would share that information with him.

"Yeah, she confided in me when she once visited me in prison. It was her way of explaining her actions. She thought I would understand, and I did, but I could not trust that she could love me genuinely. The stereotypes would always live inside her head."

"And I agree with you. I had a white female friend who became near and dear to my heart, like a soul sister. However, when she would introduce me to her family and other friends, she would mention during the introduction, *"she is not one of them; she is different,"* Then one day, she wanted this district manager position over the grocery store chain she had been working at for years. She was up against another Black woman that I did not know. Somehow, she learned the Black woman had no degree but still was awarded the job."

"Really?" Oliver questioned, taking Jamie's hand and walking again.

"Yeah, that ended our friendship simply because of her comments about the Black woman's achievement. Saying things like, the job was afraid she would pull the race card, so they gave her the job."

"And that is my point exactly. Those inner thoughts I could never detect. I just decided to move forward. It was a tough decision because Liza was cool, but something would not let me trust it."

"I get it. Enough about Liza. I want to know where you see yourself in five years?"

"Hopefully married, still running my businesses, and with at least one child."

"What if the woman you wanted to marry already had a child and did not want more children?"

"Is that you?" he asked, directing her to a park bench to sit down.

"I want more children but cannot have more since Karl, and I divorced. I do not love the idea of half-siblings. I grew up that way and want wholeness for my child."

"Then you need to reconcile with Karl because a man without children, who wants a child, will love your child and still want a child of his own."

"Yeah, but the thought of that I am not feeling. Not sure how that will change in the future, so do not get too connected to me. I do not want that to be an issue if we continue to move forward. Right now, it looks like just friends are the best for us."

Broken7

"Define friends?" he asked, moving closer to her on the bench.

"It is strictly platonic, and you can date and mess around with whomever you want. I can do the same, and loyalty will build through friendship. If you want, I will give you sound advice on the knuckleheads you date. I might ask you for advice as well. If the Lord grows us into something more than friends, it will happen on his watch, not ours."

"I really like that; it is real. It allows us to get to know each other without expectations. And it sets a tone that allows us to choose wisely. I never met a woman as confident as you are, Jamie. I think this will be great! And it allows me time to let go of Liza. I cared for her."

"Yeah, unfortunately, most other women have a different approach when they meet a man. They want to know what he wants in a woman, income, and family situation. As for me, I want to know about you. I live by naturally attract. All the other details will become known. You cannot teach it or expect it; it just works."

"Yes, that is true. I feel that same spark today as I did in Cartel's living room. You are a different breed, Jamie. Thank you for allowing us to have this time together tonight."

"Thank you for asking me out. I look forward to building a great friendship with you." She got up from the bench.

"Same here. Allow me to walk you to your car."

"I appreciate that, Mr.," she responded, allowing him to lead.

Sunday afternoon, Wren and Anna sat out in the sunroom with baby Seven, having a glass of sweet tea with cheese and crackers. Anna started to make weekly visits to see her grandson, to who she was in love and attached. Although Anna has called Wren daily, trying to connect with her since the birth of Seven, Wren still felt uneasy with her presence. It was hard to believe a person who disliked you so much and thought of you carrying her son's seed is now your best friend.

"So, Wren. Your mother, Sharon, and I have spent almost 36 hours together. From the first night, we went to dinner, to all-day shopping and eating the next day, to bible study at her home, she is a fun person. Meeting her has been a blessing to me. I realized I need to hang out with women more." Anna acknowledged.

"Yes, she always had friends hanging around our house when I was younger. Always well-liked for some reason."

"She is extraordinary. She taught me more in 36 hours than I learned from my elders, and I am older than her, but she has more knowledge."

"You think so?" Wren questioned.

"I know so. A few women in my life have challenged me to look in the mirror and honestly question my character. I never listened because I always had myself together financially, and no one could tell me anything. But when your mother asked me who my friends were, I could only say my husband. It made me think. I have lost many friends due to my arrogancy and carelessness of others' feelings."

"I can see that." Wren agreed, handing her the baby.

"Yes, I almost lost my son because I did not want to see him with you. That was the icing on the cake when he told me you were not going anywhere. God showed him he was the wrong person during the hard times. Then he said, mom. I am committed to spending the rest of my life making up to Wren. I was pissed because I did not understand the good he saw in you. I questioned God and my husband. So, then I asked myself, why is she not the one? And guess what, I could not produce an answer." Anna hugged her grandson, who smelled so good. She loved the smell of newborn babies.

Wren sat and watched Anna with amazement; she could not believe the old lady had a heart. She was so mean to her to this point. "Well, I am glad we are in a better space now."

"Me too, because your mother is phenomenal, but she also raised a remarkable daughter. You are an excellent fit for my son. I love your strong character and how you knew better than to let a man rule over you. I did not have that fight in me. I got taught the opposite. I got trained to allow the man to lead you and for you to silence to authority."

"Yeah, Casanova told me how he never thought that was right as a child watching you slave after his father. He also mentioned his dad did not think it was right either."

"That is correct; Gregory always told me to speak openly about my thoughts and opinions. He did want a mute as a wife, but that was all I learned from his mother. He soon adapted to my behavior and loved me for whom I was, but throughout life, he would periodically say, I just wish you would free yourself. The thing is, he did not know much about my upbringing. I would not share it with him. The mental and physical abuse I endured coming up in life. Last night, he just found out when I cried myself to sleep on his chest after your mother challenged me to get it off my chest."

"Wow! My mother does have a way of getting people to examine themselves. She helped me to look at Casanova differently. She allows God to use her. She is an advocate for helping broken people regain their strength."

"You mean, Yah?" Anna corrected her.

"Yes, ma'am." Wren smiled

"Yah knows what we need and when we need it. He brings us out by allowing us to receive it when it is right. Some suffer longer than others because they do not have an ear to hear. But when it is time, you are going to listen."

"I agree with you, Ms. Anna," Wren responded.

"Your mom is going to get back with Daniel. We talked about him as well. They went to dinner tonight. She is supposed to have a heart-to-heart with him, and I hope it goes well."

"Yep, she told Steven and me it was time to make amends. We told her we supported her decision to reconcile. The betrayal was real, but we understand his heart shattered."

"And he was wrong too, especially to your brother and you. But as for your mother, yes, she is doing the right thing."

"Listening to you made me think about how Yah has done so much work in me over the last months and my friends. We have endured some life-changing events. We always had it rougher than others, but we always made good. However, this time, the things we endured felt unbearable at times. Our husbands challenged us all to be in a place we had never experienced. Lessons learned for all of us."

"Yeah, how so?" Anna asked.

"I learned that living with unforgiveness in my heart limited my ability to be great. And harboring old feelings had me caged inside a hard shell until I met Casanova. He then challenged me to fight for what's right instead of allowing more wrong, hurt, and pain. I learned of Yah's love and grace and mercy through his son Yeshua, who kept me until the point of healing. I forgave my mother, stepfather, and husband and gave birth to my baby boy, Seven. He is the most handsome and innocent little face on the planet."

"He is the most handsome little guy ever." Anna hugged him again.

"Then I think about my friend; Jamie, her husband, took her through hell having a child with her sister. And before she could come to terms with that, her sister tries to kill her, eventually killing herself. Jamie's mother was a pill all her life. She had to raise her siblings, lose her marriage, and become a single parent to a beautiful baby girl."

"Her story still gives me the teary eye. That was extremely hard to endure. She, too, is a strong woman. I think I would have killed Gregory. I mean, I know I would have killed him."

"Yeah, but I have seen some happiness in her over the last week. I think her and Mr. Stickmen will hit it off eventually."

"I do not think I met him yet," Anna stated.

"No, he is new around the crew. The point is that Yah brought Jamie through it, and she reconciled with her mother. Then finally, Cartel and her fight to have a baby for years. It almost led to her husband cheating on her. To deal with that, on top of finding out your birth mother had been watching you grow up for years."

"Now that part, Yah, is good because I would've struggled with forgiving my mother especially knowing I was in foster care getting abused."

"How did you know that, Anna?"

"My son did tell me that much, but not in a gossiping way, but it was for me to forgive my mother who sold me off to men for drugs when I was a teenager. My mother is dead and gone, but I still live with unforgiveness. My son told me I would be a better person if I just forgave. I have let go and am learning to live with that said."

It was the end of Summer. Wren and Casanova invited friends and family over for a barbeque gathering. Cartel and George came along with their handsome baby boy, Elijah. Jamie and Karl were still friends and co-parenting; they were in attendance. Anna and Gregory made their way, of course. Casanova's friend, Ryan, married Ginny just two weeks prior. Everyone was shocked he had finally settled down.

Liza and Oliver remained cordial and part of the group as they developed a friendship over time. The ladies' mothers, Susan, Sharon, Cena, and Jamie's twin sisters, were attending. Sharon gave a long speech about brokenness and unapologetic as everyone ate meals and fellowshipped.

Everyone acknowledged Wren's award acceptance speech and her mom, Sharon, speech this evening; life is tough. Life is full of ups and downs, but the key is not to let it change who you are as a person unless the change is necessary to better yourself. Casanova further explained that people have to self-reflect and identify who they are and if it's who they want to be. He acknowledged getting looped into his parent's ideal of marriage almost cost him. And with that, the group ended the night with laughter, dancing, and eating more food than their stomachs allowed.

Matter of the heart discussion with Sherlynn Rachelle

The characters in this book inspired me. We live in a world that equates success to having money, professional titles, many high-value material things, beauty, etc. Truthfully those attributes are tremendous yet cause so much jealousy, envy, and self-hate in this world.

The chase of it damages friendships, marriages, and loss of time and memories with the ones you love. Once obtained, the time it takes to maintain could cause a mental and physical breakdown in the body. Mental health breakdown is rising because of the chase or jealousy of the ones who have achieved.

We are unsuccessful if we are not WHOLE in mind, body, and soul. The book of Proverbs can help us to transform our mind, body, and soul. The

Broken7

Bible teaches us not to follow the concepts of this world. And to be transformed by the renewing of our mind. Romans 12.

Medications do not heal us; they weaken us. Medications treat disease but never cure disease. Holding pain inside; damages us. Healing comes from speaking out and facing it. Make-up doesn't heal us; beauty lies from within.

My goal is to live a life of wholeness, and I pray that everyone who reads this book joins this plan of action. Love yourself, and do great for yourself. Be a blessing to all the Lord discerns you to bless. And to love hard, the ones who love you. Always be mindful and respectful of others. Daily prayer and worship will contribute to a better you.

All Praises to The Most High, Father of Jesus (Yeshua) Christ. I hope to chat with you soon and that you & I will continue to be lifelong reading buddies.

Blessings & Love, In Spirit and Truth,

Sherlynn Rachelle

www.ingramcontent.com/pod-product-compliance
Lightning Source LLC
Chambersburg PA
CBHW031425200626

46814CB00016B/1674